IN-FLIGHT ENTERTAINMENT

IN-FLIGHT
ENTERTAINMENT

Stories

HELEN SIMPSON

 ALFRED A. KNOPF · New York · 2012

THIS IS A BORZOI BOOK
PUBLISHED BY ALFRED A. KNOPF

Originally published in Great Britain by Jonathan Cape, an
imprint of the Random House Group Limited, London, in 2010.

The stories in this collection were originally published in the
following: "In-Flight Entertainment," "Scan," and "Sorry?"
in Granta; *"Squirrel," "Homework," and "Diary of an*
Interesting Year" (also published in The Sunday Times*) in*
The New Yorker; *"I'm Sorry but I'll Have to Let You Go" and*
"Charm for a Friend with a Lump" in Good Housekeeping;
"Geography Boy" in The Sunday Times; *"Ahead of the Pack,"*
"The Tipping Point," and "Channel 17" (also published in
The Guardian*) in* Zoetrope; *and "The Festival of the Immortals"*
in The Guardian.

Library of Congress Cataloging-in-Publication Data
Simpson, Helen, 1957–
In-flight entertainment : stories / by Helen Simpson. — 1st ed.
p. cm.
"This is a Borzoi book."
ISBN 978-0-307-59558-4
I. Title
PR6069.I4226I54 2012
823'.914—dc23   2011040331

Jacket photograph by Charlie Surbey/Gallery Stock
Jacket design by Gabriele Wilson
Manufactured in the United States of America

FIRST UNITED STATES EDITION

Contents

IN-FLIGHT ENTERTAINMENT

In-Flight Entertainment

After all that nonsense at Heathrow, it came as particularly welcome to find himself upgraded to first class. This hadn't happened to Alan before and he looked round him with beady pleasure. Business Class he was used to, Club Class and Premium Economy and what have you, the extra eight inches were a lifesaver when you were six foot plus; but not First, until now.

His champagne was in a real glass rather than a plastic facsimile. It made a difference. He had way more room to stretch his legs, and on a nine-hour trip to Chicago that counted for something, especially after a four-hour delay. The big armchairs were ranged in curved couples, like Victorian love seats; his own faced forward, while the old guy opposite had the window seat of this pair, its back to the cockpit. They were near enough to converse if they chose, but so far hadn't done so, which suited Alan just fine.

The other First-Class passengers were mainly business types like himself, or much older men. No women, unless you counted the air stewardesses. His own stopped and smiled at him fondly, so he took another sparkle-filled glass from her tray. He could get used to this. Yes, really quite old; the passenger just across the aisle from him, for example: he must be eighty if he was a day, and not looking too good on it, either. Cabin crew had already had to help him totter down the aisle to the toilet, first one in after the seat-belt signs went off, and even now he couldn't seem to settle; he'd just pressed the button for more attention Alan couldn't help but notice.

Yes, he was going to enjoy this flight, he decided, inspecting the menu and the list of films on offer. He was a bit of a film buff. Something retro to start with, something easy to eat by; here it was, just the thing, *North by Northwest* with Cary Grant and Eva Marie Saint. King prawns on a bed of wild rice with star anise. Already he was aware of his tightening facial skin and sore red eyes but this could hardly be called an ordeal. It's being up in the clouds, he thought, as the champagne kicked in; it's being in transit. I'm where it's at.

All you needed for the modern world was to know

how to work a remote control—when to fast-forward, when to double-click—which was something these older guys simply couldn't get the hang of. The screen on the swivel arm in front of him showed a shrunken globe with a jewel of an airplane—the one he was on—just clear of the tiny triangle that represented the U.K., at the start of its journey across the pond. He felt unaccountably moved. The end of the world was nigh, that's what the Heathrow nutters had been shouting, basically. Global warming, he was sick of the sound of it, he only had to see those words and a massive wave of boredom engulfed him.

Even his parents had jumped on the bandwagon, nattering on about their carbon footprints the last time he went to see them, complaining about how the lawn needed mowing right through winter now, showing off their new wiggly lightbulbs. His mother had sneaked a sticker onto the bumper of his new Merc SUV—"Costing the Earth." He hadn't noticed, but Penny had been furious when she'd seen it.

"Your mother," she'd hissed. "She'd like us all to go back to saving little bits of string, just like *her* mother did in the war. That does it: I'm not having her over here being holier-than-thou about the patio heaters."

The old guy across the aisle was making quite a fuss now; Alan watched his freckled baldy head jerking round and his hands fluttering spasmodically as the stewardess leaned down to ask him what he wanted.

She was nice, that girl, a nice smile and nice teeth; though she wasn't smiling now, right enough. What a job! You had to hand it to them.

The thing was, as he'd tried to explain to his parents, the science behind these new reports could be quite shaky. There were two sides to every coin, and anyway Planet Earth has a self-regulating mechanism, rather like the economy, and we should leave it to right itself. Mother Nature knows a thing or two, he'd told them, tapping his nose; don't you worry. And if it does get too hot, America's going to send giant mirrors into space to deflect some of the sun's rays back off into the darkness. "What about the polar bears," his mother had persisted. She'd always preferred animals to humans, as she proudly announced from time to time. "Yes, it's a shame about the polar bears," Alan had said, growing exasperated. "And the three-toed Amazonian tree frogs. But there you go. It's the survival of the fittest out there, Mum."

"Last time we came to meet you at the airport," his father had butted in, apropos of nothing in particular that Alan could see, "there was this American family and the kids were all in T-shirts saying, 'Darwin Was Wrong.' "

Where was the food? He was going to go for the *boeuf en croûte* rather than the Indonesian fish curry. More of the cabin crew seemed to have converged now on the old man with his fluttering hands. The nice stewardess flashed Alan a smile when he caught her eye, then went back to looking worried. An announcement came out over the sound system for any doctor on board to please come forward. Now, for the first time, Alan's opposite number in the curving double seat leaned across and spoke to him.

"I can't see what's going on from here," he rasped.

"It's the old guy in the next seat along," whispered Alan. "He seems to be in some sort of trouble. Oh look, here's someone. Must be a doctor. He's obviously not best pleased. Now they're making the seat recline. They've got him lying down flat."

Other heads too were craning to get a look at the drama. The cabin crew stuck determined smiles on their faces and started to do the rounds, taking orders for dinner.

"Four hours' delay," volunteered Alan. "Thanks to those jokers at Heathrow. Alan Barr, by the way."

"And I'm Jeremy Lees. Yes, those anti-flying protesters. A waste of time."

"Complete time wasters."

"I suppose so," said Jeremy. "What I meant, though, was, it was a waste of *their* time. They're not going to change anything."

"Exactly. It's nonsense, isn't it, this global warming stuff. Trying to turn the wheel back. Half the scientists don't agree with it anyway."

"Actually I think you'll find they do. Ah, red

please," said Jeremy as the air stewardess offered him wine. "What have you got? Merlot or Zinfandel? I'll try the Zinfandel. Thank you. No, they do agree now, they've reached a consensus; I ought to know, I was one of them. No, it's not nonsense, I'm afraid. The world really is warming up."

"Merlot," said Alan, rather annoyed. These finger-wagging types were getting everywhere. Even his own firm had been pressured into signing up for some carbon-offsetting scheme recently. An extra £19.50 it had cost for this trip to Chicago. Plant a bloody tree. All a big con trick. "So how long have we got?" he demanded with a tinge of belligerence. "Cheers."

"Your health," replied Jeremy, raising his glass in a courtly manner. "Well. They *were* saying thirty years, but now it's looking more like twenty, or even fifteen. Still, that should see me out."

Old bugger, thought Alan; how self-centered can you get. The children'll be in their twenties.

"The thing is, the nearer you get to a mountain, the less of it you see," said Jeremy obscurely. "Like old people and death."

Enough of you, thought Alan, nodding at him and donning his headphones. Cary Grant was waiting at a bus stop in the Midwest, and in the distance was the little crop-spraying plane buzzing toward him. He hadn't really noticed it yet. This was the best bit of the film; Alan couldn't help losing concentration though when he noticed from the corner of his eye that his favorite air stewardess was holding a plastic bag of liquid aloft. She was standing just ahead of him in the aisle, while a man who was presumably the passenger-doctor had started to fit a drip. A second stewardess held a flashlight. Wow, thought Alan; it must be serious. He looked round again, uneasy. He could see a man playing Sudoku, and another forking food into his mouth like there was no tomorrow.

Nobody else seemed bothered.

"It's getting serious over there," he said, pulling off his headphones and addressing Jeremy in a low voice. From the corner of his eye he could see Cary Grant running for his life.

"Oh?" said Jeremy.

"They've rigged up a drip," said Alan. "It all looks a bit DIY. One of them's shining a flashlight. You don't think they'll try to, uh, operate?"

"Extremely unlikely," said Jeremy. "Not the right conditions for that, really. Think of the litigation, too—it would take a brave doctor these days to operate; particularly in First Class to America."

Alan looked back at the furtive drama playing itself out across the aisle, at the hot unhappy faces of the participating cabin crew. The doctor pushed down rhythmically, with pauses, straight-armed and grim. CPR, thought Alan, recognizing the process from countless episodes of *Casualty* and *ER*.

"This is your captain speaking," came the aircraft sound system. "Unfortunately, as some of you are already aware, one of our passengers has been taken ill and needs more help than we can provide on board. Accordingly, we have arranged to land at the next available opportunity in order to provide this passenger with the medical attention he needs. We will be landing at Goose Bay in approximately two hours."

"Goose Bay!" said Alan. "Where the hell's that?"

There was a murmur of discomfiture all round him, a general raising of eyebrows, and a barrage of discreet but questioning looks directed at the ongoing life-and-death spectacle.

"It's in Labrador," said Jeremy.

"How far is that from Quebec?" asked Alan. "Montreal?"

"Oh, hundreds of miles," said Jeremy. "It's north of Newfoundland. We'll be up near Greenland, or what's left of it."

Alan swore softly to himself. Four hours' delay at Heathrow, now this. He had to give his presentation in exactly thirteen hours' time. Great.

"Anyway, I'll tell you why there's no point in us trying to cut back on carbon emissions and all the rest of it," he snapped at Jeremy, aware that he was allowing himself to slide into a rage. "In a word, pal—China!"

"China," said Jeremy, mildly amused. "Yes, yes, the Yellow Peril."

"If everyone in China gets on a plane, we're screwed," said Alan.

"Agreed. Though do remember they've only got four hundred or so airports at the moment, as opposed to five thousand plus in America." He turned to the air stewardess at his side. "I'll have the Swiss white chocolate pavé, please, with the Tayside raspberry coulis."

There was a flurry across the aisle and Alan craned his neck to make out the doctor arming himself with some sort of wired machine. *Whump,* it went; *whump, whump.* Pause. Alan saw the old man's hands fly up in the air and come down again.

"What's that?" he asked the air stewardess with a jerk of his head. Her eyes were suspiciously watery despite her professional smile. She shook her head and moved away.

"That'll be the defibrillator," said Jeremy.

Alan realized she had failed to take his pudding order and wondered if he could call her back. Probably not a good idea under the circumstances. Now Cary Grant was climbing up Washington's granite nose. Pudding was the best part of the meal for him. He allowed himself to be distracted by the Mount Rushmore chase sequence for a few minutes, and the next time he looked up he saw the doctor shaking his head and rolling down his sleeves. Did that mean . . . ? Apparently it did, because a tartan blanket was being pulled up over what must now be the corpse.

Jeez. It made you think.

"Jeremy," he said, after a few seconds, leaning across. "Er, something's *happened* over there, I think." Jeremy looked up from his book, sharp eyes greatly intensified for a moment by the lenses of his glasses. He peered at Alan.

"He's gone, then?" he said.

"Incredible," said Alan. "I don't believe it. Right beside us."

"Oh, I've seen it before on airplanes," said Jeremy. "It happens more than you might think, particularly in First Class. If they're taken ill in Economy, they're brought through here because there's more space. Quite a cause of bad feeling sometimes."

"How so?" asked Alan, shocked.

"Well, people don't want to pay out several thousand for a ticket and then find they have to sit beside a dead body all the way to Hong Kong."

Alan glanced involuntarily at the shape beneath the blanket. Put like that. Hardly ideal. Still, the poor guy.

"The poor guy," he said, reprovingly. "Looks like he was on his own, too. Far from home and family. Poor guy!"

"Maybe," said Jeremy. "Or maybe it was as good a way to go as any—quick, up in the clouds, helped on his way by kind cabin crew. Certainly better than a hospice or a geriatric ward or at home alone in front of *Countdown.*"

Weirdo, thought Alan. He drew back into his broad winged chair. It was unsettling, all this. Next thing he felt a tap on his shoulder and turned round to the inquiring face of the Sudoku man sitting across the aisle behind him.

"Do you think," asked the man, "do you think we'll still have to land at Goose Bay now that, er?"

"That's a point," said Alan.

"We're almost six hours behind schedule as it is," said the man, tapping his watch.

"You're right."

"Because there's nothing they'll be able to do for him in Goose Bay."

"No," said Alan. "With the best will in the world."

"Exactly."

When they asked the air hostess about this a little later, however, she told them that they still *would* have to land there, as the request had been acted upon by air traffic control, it was all logged in and un-deprogrammable.

Once they were stationary on Goose Bay's landing strip, it became apparent that they would be stuck there for quite some while. A coroner had to be found before the body could be taken off the plane, and tracking down a coroner in Goose Bay in the middle of the night was proving difficult.

"No," said Jeremy when Alan inquired, "this hasn't happened to me before. The other deaths took less time, I suppose, and the flights carried on to their destinations. No, I haven't had to make an unscheduled landing like this before."

Great, thought Alan, staring furiously through the little airplane window. Outside was a desolate runway and a couple of hangars with corrugated iron roofs. It was snowing heavily.

"Think of the problems for his next of kin," said Jeremy. "Having to fly here and identify the body. Repatriation won't be the easiest thing to organize from Goose Bay, one imagines."

"We're in the middle of nowhere," snapped Alan. "Ridiculous. Look at that weather. Don't tell me you still believe in global warming—it's fucking freezing out there."

"It's not a question of belief," said Jeremy. "It's happened. It's happening."

"Not out there," snorted Alan. "Not from what I can see."

"In fact, someone really should declare a global state of emergency, given the evidence. The scientists are quaking in their boots."

"There's your so-called evidence," said Alan, now in an evil temper. "Look at that snow. If we hang round here for much longer they'll find it's impossible to take off."

"Don't worry," soothed Jeremy. "I won't preach. I used to try to explain it to everyone I met, but last year I could see that it was futile, so I gave up. After all, it's quite an unpleasant chunk of information to absorb."

"So what *do* you think will happen?"

"No, no, I don't want to bore you."

"I'm asking, pal."

"Oh, in *that* case. Well, it'll all get very nasty."

"We'll be swimming round the Statue of Liberty's torch," sneered Alan. "I saw that film."

"No, no," said Jeremy. "Crops will fail first. Food shortages will kill off four-fifths of the population, along with malaria and bird flu and so on. There'll be warlords and fighting in the streets. By the time you're my age you'll be beating them off your vegetable patch and your last tins of tuna."

"Super," said Alan.

"And don't think you'll be able to escape by moving to Canada," Jeremy continued playfully. "That's where the Americans will go; it's the same continent, after all, and lots of them are buying up real estate in this sort of area even now. No, you'll probably have to make your way back to bonny Scotland and hope for the best."

"Oh cheers," said Alan. "And what about you? You don't seem too worried yourself, I can't help noticing."

"No," agreed Jeremy. "I think you'll find most people over seventy are the same—at some level we're banking on current fuel stocks to see us out. By the time rationing comes in, it'll all be someone else's problem."

"So you're all right Jack!" snorted Alan.

"I'll tell you when I stopped trying to change things. It was when I realized that nothing was going to stop people from flying."

"Are you saying I shouldn't *fly* now?"

"I don't care what you do," said Jeremy peaceably. "I don't care about you. You don't care about me. We don't care about *him*." He gestured in the direction of the dead man. "We all know how to put ourselves first, and that's what makes the world go round."

"Because I'm a frequent flier," insisted Alan. "My job requires me to fly in excess of fifty thousand miles a year."

"I wouldn't boast about that when the floods come," said Jeremy, "or you'll find yourself strung up from the nearest lamppost. No, self-interest is usually the most efficient form of insurance, but it doesn't seem to be working here. You and nearly everybody else are such scientific ignoramuses that you can't take on board what's about to wipe you out."

"You seem very sure that you're right about everything," said Alan nastily.

"Not really," said Jeremy. "But I am about this."

Just my luck, thought Alan, to get stuck with a moralizing old wise guy in the middle of nowhere.

"We need heat and light and food for survival," continued Jeremy. "We don't *need* to fly. But nobody's going to give up flying, because it's the biggest perk of modern life—so cheap and fast and easy."

"You'd rather," said Alan loudly, "you'd rather keep it only for the *rich,* eh? You're just being elitist."

"Elitist!" laughed Jeremy. "You're the elitist, Alan. Even if you were dragged up on the meanest of shoe-strings through your recent gadget-ridden childhood, you're still one of the world's rich. It's us rich ones that jet round the globe guzzling untaxed jet fuel and plowing up the stratosphere like there's no tomorrow."

"I took my family snorkeling in the Maldives last year," said Alan, "and all the people we met there were one hundred percent dependent on our holidays for their livelihood. *Lovely* people they were. What about them? Tourism employs almost one in ten people worldwide, did you know that? Do you want *them* to starve?"

"Ha! The Maldives are about to go under, literally, and how will their people live then?"

"That's nothing to do with flying. Airplanes are a drop in the ocean compared to all the other stuff."

"I'm afraid you're laboring under a misapprehension there, Alan. Flying is far and away the fastest-growing source of man-made greenhouse gases."

"Yeah, yeah."

"Over two billion people flew last year, even though ninety-five percent of the world's population has never been on a plane," continued Jeremy, imperturbable. "So a few people are flying a *lot.* But it's the non-fliers who are first in line to pay the price."

"*We're* getting floods too," said Alan, aggressive, defensive.

"And it doesn't look like we'll be voting for constraints on our flying until there's mass death at home. First to go under will be Bangladesh, but until Miami and Sydney join it we're not only not going to stop flying, we're not going to fly less, either. In fact, quite the opposite—we're all set to fly more. Much more."

"You're right there, at least," said Alan, yawning and stretching.

"Listen, you can turn off your mobile phone charger and drive an electric car and all the rest of it, but if you take just one flight a year you'll cancel all the savings you've made. Flying is *incredibly* harmful to the atmosphere. Haven't you even heard of contrails?"

"You're on a road to nowhere," smiled Alan. "The aircraft industry is where it's at. Mega growth predicted. It's set to triple in the next twenty years; it's going through the roof."

"Yes. I know."

"Heathrow will get its third runway anytime now."

"Good for you. Nowhere else on the planet are the

skies as crowded as over London and the South East. That must make you very happy. Now, I wonder where this coroner can be? By my calculation we've been in Goose Bay for nearly three hours."

"Unbelievable," said Alan with a seismic yawn. "I cannot believe this journey. We're going to be stuck here forever, frozen to the tarmac."

"They'll discover us in a million years' time, the archaeologists," said Jeremy. "A perfectly preserved fossil from the late carboniverous period."

At this point the coroner arrived, scowling and disheveled, trailed by four big sullen stretcher bearers in plaid shirts.

"He looks like they had to drag him out of a bar," said Alan, watching as the man was led to the shape beneath the blanket. "He looks well over the limit."

"The limit is probably higher in Goose Bay," said Jeremy, surveying the cheerless scene outside. "And who can wonder."

Red-eyed, dehydrated and exhausted, Alan declined the next glass of champagne and ordered a black coffee. They were up in the air again. About bloody time. Less than two hours until he set foot on American soil. He couldn't wait. He missed its lavish confidence and grandeur, the twelve-lane highways of gigantic cars, the insouciance with which his friends there used planes like buses. Hell, loads of them commuted by plane every day, Burbank to L.A., that sort of thing. They just got on and did things; they were always coming up with something new. Think of last year and the heated sidewalks in that ski resort in Colorado.

It was a real problem these days, finding a decent skiing holiday. Europe was useless. Penny was suggesting Dubai for next year. She'd heard it had guaranteed meter-deep snow everywhere, real snow topped up every night; and the shopping there was amazing, too, the Mall of the Emirates was right next door to the ski dome. It occurred to him that Jeremy would probably disapprove of this too, which made him angry again.

"What I can't understand," he said unpleasantly, leaning over the seat divider, "with all due respect, Jeremy, is, why are you even *on* this plane? If you think flying's so bad, why are you *here?*"

"Might as well be." Jeremy shrugged. "Once I realized the world's going to hell in a handcart—or, rather, in a Boeing 747, or on an Airbus or a Dreamliner—I thought, Might as well. Haven't you noticed the old people at airports? All those beeping cartloads of us with our replacement hips and knees? It gets us out of the house, and we don't care about the delays because it makes the time we've got left seem longer."

"Oh," said Alan, taken aback.

"Plus," said Jeremy slowly, "I wouldn't mind joining the other Mile High Club. Eventually."

"The other *what?*"

"Well, I am already a member of the original Mile High Club. Believe it or not. I was enrolled a few decades ago under a blanket in Business Class with the girl next door, so to speak. It's not humanly possible in Economy; you'd have to go off for a tryst in the toilet, and call me an old romantic but that never appealed. Business Class is fine, though, if you're good at keeping quiet."

"What do you mean, the *other* Mile High Club?" said Alan, gawping at him.

"The one our friend's just joined," said Jeremy.

"What friend?"

"You know. The one we left behind in Goose Bay."

"You mean . . . ?"

"Yes. A more distinguished way to go, don't you think? Nearer to heaven, and so on."

"Oh," said Alan. He couldn't believe his ears. He couldn't think of anything to say. He stretched his eyes at Jeremy, then gave a weak smile and feigned sleep behind a padded satin eye mask.

Sleep would not come to him, however. Pictures of Scotland danced behind his eyelids. Raspberry canes in the rain. Gloom and doom. Tatties and neeps. Penny and the kids were turning their noses up. Barbed wire round his allotment, right enough. A big solid house near the Cairngorms, with a view of Ben Macdhui or Braeriach. He'd better buy a dinghy. A gun. That should hold them off for a while, until . . . Until *what*?

A cataclysmic snort from his own nasal cavity shocked him awake.

"Coffee, sir?"

He took a cup before he was quite compos mentis, then sipped as he stared, sore-eyed, at their on-screen progress. The airplane-jewel was nearly at the gold dot marked Chicago. The Atlantic had been left behind, along with the frozen wastes of Goose Bay. They were high above Earth, zooming along at five hundred miles an hour. Of course he accepted this on a superficial level, but deep down he did not believe it. It was like when the physics teacher had tried to explain about magnetism, or when he'd told them that everything was really bundles of atoms holding hands. Pull the other one!

All the alarmist crap that old creep Jeremy had been coming out with, it just seemed like a fairy story now. He wasn't a six-year-old to believe in magic. Nothing but hot air. He drained his coffee cup and handed it back to the air stewardess.

It was a relief when the announcement was made that they were approaching their destination. At last, he thought. This journey had been a nightmare. When all was said and done, though, they'd made it, and he was still in time to give his presentation, even if there wouldn't be any chance to drop his bags off first at the hotel.

He tended to look forward to the seat-belts-on

preparations for landing; he approved of how, with the flight's end in sight, the cabin crew became newly purposeful and bright-eyed. In quite a childish way he liked the tiny brightly wrapped bonbons, he liked yawning to pop his ears. Yes, his spirits usually lifted during the descent, and he would have expected to feel extra jubilant toward the close of this particular protracted crossing. Right now though, as they made their approach to O'Hare, he noticed that his spirits were not in fact responding with their usual ebullience. No. Instead, he felt somehow unnerved, he had a weight round his heart, a nasty sinking feeling; which was not like him at all.

Squirrel

Gardening!" said the girl, and tilted back in her chair the way she knew would get a reaction. "It's like knitting, isn't it."

"Stop that, Lara," said her mother, "You'll break the chair."

"A sign of middle age," continued Lara. "*Old* age. It's what *old* people do when there's nothing left in their lives."

"I thought you were supposed to be learning Henry VIII," said her mother, Susan, glaring at her over a recently acquired pair of Ready Readers.

"Look at him, snipping away," said Lara and pointed to her father up the garden with his pruning shears.

"You're just control freaks, you two. You should let it run wild!"

"Right," grunted Susan, returning to her list.

"You could have a meadow out there," persisted Lara. "Go green. A jungle!"

"It might just as well be," said Susan. "Great fat lumps of squirrels crashing through the trees like monkeys. Come on, Lara, what about some studying."

"Don't tell me what to do!" shrieked Lara.

"Perish the thought," said Susan. "But if you're going to take over the kitchen table like this when you've got a perfectly good desk in your bedroom . . ."

"Listen to me," hissed Lara. "What I'm putting myself through here is entirely voluntary. It's not necessary, it's *my* choice. All the clever people are setting up Internet businesses, they're not wasting their time on this, they wouldn't dream of doing this. They're going to be millionaires in five years' time. And I'll be in debt, twenty thousand, thirty thousand . . ."

Her mobile ringtone cut in, a jaunty jerky samba, and instantly she was transported from cold-eyed fury to smiles and coos of delight. "Really . . . *really*. . . . No, she's so not like that. . . . Oh, that's so funny. . . ." One artless peal of laughter after another unloosed itself into the air.

Susan stared out the window into the green and white of May. I'm the family whipping boy, she thought. How moody it was, the weather: hormonal, melodramatic, lurching from thunder to glaring sun and back again in the space of an hour. She had been out there earlier, before breakfast, the whispering air blowing through the hairs on her skin. This sudden lush frondescence was springing up at the rate of an inch a day at least; you could stop and watch it grow like an erection. Efficient speedy impersonal sex: just what she hadn't wanted at Lara's age. She must stop seeing him. On the other hand, she didn't want to. The office was another world. It had nothing to do with them.

"That was Ruby," said Lara as she finished her call.

"How is Ruby these days? Now that she's split up with—Sean, was it?"

"Oh, she hasn't split up with him. She doesn't trust him, but that doesn't mean she's split up with him. No, she's made him give her the password to his Hotmail so she can check it anytime she likes."

"Wow," said Susan.

"Careful, Dad!" said Lara, as Barry came in from the garden and sat down beside her. "Mind my notes."

He doesn't know my password, Susan reminded herself, glancing at her husband.

"I've caught one of the little buggers," he said, patting Lara's arm in triumph. "I've trapped it under a dustbin lid and I've put bricks on top."

"What little buggers?" said Lara.

"A squirrel."

At least they were united in their detestation of squirrels, thought Susan. Earlier this year they had stamped across the grass and wrung their hands together over the scores of nibbled white camellia buds that had been scattered over the lawn like popcorn. Barry had started to talk longingly about rat traps. "Clean, quick, humane," he had mused. "A metal jaw comes down on the neck and all but decapitates them." He had an explosive temper, just as Lara did. The two of them were tinderbox touchy, gigantically flinty. She was sick of acting as the lightning rod for all their casual rage.

"Of all the things in the world to get upset about, you choose squirrels," said Lara. "What about climate change? Why don't you get upset about that instead? My children will fry, thanks to your minibreaks."

"I should cut its head off and stick it on a spike," said Barry, ruffling his daughter's hair. "Like Henry VIII did with traitors."

He doesn't know, thought Susan. He doesn't know.

"That's so cruel!" said Lara, looking up at him from under her eyelashes. "You're not really going to kill it, are you?"

"I don't know what to do." He shrugged. "Nothing else seems to stop them."

"The law says you have to drive any squirrel you catch far out into woodland," said Susan.

"And kill it then?" said Lara. "Like Snow White?"

"No," said Susan. "Then you set it free."

"Well, I'm buggered if I'm going to spend my Saturday taking a squirrel on its holidays," said Barry. "By the way, Susan, I thought you were going to organize some more potting compost. We've almost run out."

Susan looked at the two of them, side by side at the table. Barry was fair but with a high Saxon color and narrow hot blue eyes that gave him an intermittently dangerous look. Lara was fair too, but fairer than her father by far, with white-blond hair and such fine white skin that her features showed in her face like fruit, a mouth that brought cherries to mind or, when she yawned, strawberries. Not for the first time Susan marveled at how her own supposedly dominant genes—brown eyes, dark hair and the rest of it—hadn't stood a chance against his. Her side of the family—a pack of devious troublemaking shortarses as Barry had described them one Boxing Day on the long drive home from Lostwithiel—still muttered seventeen years on about the unlikelihood of her marriage to this outspoken Mancunian with his tendency to put on weight and throw it round.

"Henry VIII was a bully," said Susan. "He had piggy little eyes and a nasty temper. It's all coming back to me."

"Absolute power corrupts—" started Barry loftily.

"Absolutely," Lara cut in.

"The thing about tyrants is, they're vain and they like to show off," said Susan. "Didn't he have a wrestling match with Francis I? And they're short. Hitler. Napoleon. Stalin wore platform shoes."

"Henry VIII wasn't *short*," said Barry. "He was a fine figure of a man."

He puffed out his chest and placed the backs of his hands against his bulky waist, so that his arms were akimbo.

"You are like so irritating," snapped Lara. "All the people your age, the old people, they think history's like it was in their day. But it's much harder now."

"Divorced, beheaded, died," chanted Barry, "divorced, beheaded, survived. He divorced the old one from Spain, didn't he, and the ugly one, the Flanders mare. And he cut the heads off the ones who betrayed him."

Even if he has sensed something might be going on, thought Susan, he won't want to know.

"It's not like that anymore," insisted Lara, furious. "That wifey stuff's for kids. It's all lithurgy and transubstantiation now."

"Liturgy."

"Whatever."

"Anne Boleyn kept him waiting seven years," said Susan. "He wrote 'Greensleeves' for her. Then she had a baby *girl* not a son and heir, so he said, Off with her head. But he still loved her a bit, which is why he paid for the finest swordsman in France to come over and do the job."

"It wasn't because she had a girl," said Barry, with a sideways look. "It was because she was an adulteress."

Susan faltered for a second.

"Lollards," she said.

"What about them," said Barry.

We've not used mobiles at all, she thought, her mind scampering round wildly. We've only ever used e-mail and he doesn't know my password. My computer's at the office, he has no access to my e-mails, and even if he were to pick up my BlackBerry he doesn't know how to use it.

"Weren't they something to do with transubstantiation?" she said.

"No," he said.

He fixed her with his beady blue eye. He's bluffing, she told herself.

"In 1538 John Lambert was burnt at the stake," chanted Lara, holding her hand in the air to silence them, "because he held that the body of Christ wasn't substantially present during the Eucharist. Transubstantiation."

"Catholics still believe that," said Barry. "That the bread turns into Christ's body. Literally."

"But they're not allowed to believe in condoms," said Lara.

"What?" said Barry, and suddenly he was blushing like a maiden. "Lara, would you make me a cup of tea, please, while I try and decide what to do with the prisoner."

"Prisoner?" said Susan.

"The squirrel," he reminded her.

Me, thought Susan.

"What did your last slave die of," said Lara, getting up from her notes. As she filled the kettle she started to sing: " 'Alas, my love, you do me wrong, to cast me off discourteously . . .' "

It seemed to Susan that Barry was staring at her.

" 'When I have lovèd you so long, / delighting in your company,' " sang Lara. "That's your only song, Mum. You used to sing it to me to get me to sleep. Every night, 'Greensleeves.' "

"Yes," said Susan.

This was rubbing it in. If she was going to feel guilty, this would make her feel it, hearing her seventeen-year-old daughter carolling her password. Stupid choice, really: too obvious. Perhaps Barry had been tapping in all along. But she didn't feel guilty at all. It was none of his business. She only didn't want to get caught.

"I could nail it to the trellis," said Barry meditatively. "Once I've killed it, of course."

"Why would you do that?" asked Susan. "Nail it to the trellis?"

"As a warning to the other little buggers," said Barry.

"It doesn't work," said Susan. "Capital punishment as a deterrent. They've proved it. It doesn't put anybody off."

"Hung, drawn and quartered," said Lara, back at the table. "What does *that* mean?"

"Isn't that when they tie your legs and arms to four horses?" said Barry, taking a sip. "Then send them off in different directions?"

"Ugh!" said Lara, transfixed.

"No," said Susan. "That was another thing they did."

"Hanging was for commoners," said Barry. "Beheading was for the aristocracy. They still have beheadings in Saudi."

"Really," said Susan.

"When they hold the head up afterward, there are a few seconds when it, you know, the head, can actually see the crowd," said Barry. "There's enough oxygen left in the brain for it to carry on for another ten seconds."

"Right," said Susan. "Come on, Lara, back to the grindstone. You've done hardly any work this morning."

"You are so annoying!" cried Lara. "Why can't you just leave me ALONE? Why do you always have to spoil everything?"

"You won't pass if you don't get down to it. I could test you if you'd like."

"Bug off!" yelled Lara. "You think you can say anything you like to me, you don't leave me any privacy."

Privacy, thought Susan, I'll have some of that. Privacy. Whatever you like to call it.

"Look, Lara, we'll leave you alone in here if you're really going to do some work," said Barry. "Won't we, Susan. Come on, I want you to come and help me decide what to do with the culprit."

"Oh," said Susan. "All right."

The kitchen door opened onto a small square paved area planted with pots of daisies and sage and rosemary. Against the side wall was a self-assembly cold frame where they were hardening off adolescent geranium cuttings for planting out toward the end of the month. Nearby stood a bush of peonies with big pink faces, amorous and Elizabethan in their high-colored finery. Barry took her hand and held it to his mouth, kissed her fingertips, then took them in his mouth and tightened his teeth on them until she said, "Ouch" and pulled away.

"It's behind the shed, is it?" she said.

"Weighed down by bricks."

"Have you decided what to do?"

"Well, I was hoping you'd come up with an idea."

"Ah," she said carefully. There was a pause. Susan

examined the toe of her shoe. "That depends on whether you want to kill it," she continued. "And if you do, you'll upset Lara, I ought to warn you now. She'll call you cruel and murderer and all the names under the sun."

"What are your favorite flowers?" he asked. "I'd like to grow them for you."

"You should know," she said. "You should know what my favorite flowers are by now."

"I know I should, but I don't."

They walked hand in hand to the garden shed, and there behind it was a galvanized steel dustbin lid under a dozen or so bricks.

"Well?" he said.

"Roses," she replied. "But not just any old roses."

"No, of course not," he snorted.

Well, don't think I'm going to tell you after *that,* she thought; but it's those small soft damask roses I like best, with their strong sweet scent and crumpled faces in old-fashioned shades of crimson. But that'll have to stay my secret now too, won't it.

"The moment of truth," said Barry, holding down the fluted dustbin lid by its handle while he nudged the piled bricks off with his foot.

He lifted one side of the lid a couple of inches. There was no sign of movement. He lifted it another couple of inches and bent down to peer underneath. Then, like a waiter removing the domed silver cloche from a plate of roast beef, he whipped the lid into the air with a flourish. His mouth dropped open.

"It's gone!" he said. "It's gone!'

"So," said Susan, breathing again, deep into her stomach.

"No, really, Susan, I caught it. It was there. It was very small, it was a young one, but it was there. It must have scrabbled its way out somehow."

"A figment of your imagination," insisted Susan with cruel increasing confidence.

"How could I imagine a squirrel?"

"Lara's right," she said. "You're obsessed."

"You don't believe me, do you," he said helplessly.

She lifted his hand and dropped a kiss on it. Then she turned and wandered back down the garden, singing under her breath.

I'm Sorry but I'll Have to Let You Go

Hard to believe but at twenty-four he was already a Management Consultant, though of course Keats had lived life to the max by that age and Alexander the Great was leading an army against the world at fifteen. He had been living for the past year in a mansion flat in Battersea with his girlfriend, who was twenty-three and in Human Resources.

Now it was time for promotion. He had flown out to New York twice in the last fortnight, for interviews. The job offer had arrived yesterday—two years in New York starting in three months' time. It was just what should have happened, and he was satisfied. Yessss! He liked it when hard work paid off. Everything was going according to plan, like on a graph showing the ideal trajectory of a career in management consultancy.

It was a pity about Sarah. They got on well, he really quite enjoyed living with her despite the aggravation to do with picking up towels and so on; plus, she had a great bum. But she was in the end not by any means what you might call special—"the One"—and anyway it was totally the wrong moment for all that, which would be in about ten to twelve years' time. Commitment. (She couldn't even spell it, he'd noticed, spotting the central double *t* on one of her press releases, even though she was so keen to talk about it.)

But after all they had had a year together, slightly more if you counted the time before she'd moved into his flat—which he would rent out during his time in New York, it was sufficiently up to scratch to attract some sort of corporate tenant. He thought he would go for Paxman Utley rather than Shergood & Bentley, they seemed a bit sharper generally on the rental side of things, a shade more upmarket, and he'd haggle with them about that extra half percent.

So yesterday he had thought it through and decided it was only fair to give Sarah as much notice as he could about their relationship. That would give her time to adjust, also to find herself somewhere else to live. Nobody could say three months was unreasonable. There was no need to hurry things; they had plenty of time to wind it down. But it was only fair, he thought, returning to those words with satisfaction, congratulating himself on his fairness.

And this morning he had told her about the job. She asked whether he intended to accept it, which slightly threw him. Of course he did. It was the next step— she knew that.

"Don't worry," he said, hugging her in the hall and glancing at his watch. "There's loads of time. Three months. But it's very sad that we—our relationship— will, well, that it will, have to, change."

"How d'you mean?"

"Well obviously," he said. "If I'm going to be living in New York. You're not presumably imagining a transatlantic affair. It's a killer, that flight; you get worse jet lag coming back from New York than you do from twice the distance in San Francisco."

"What?"

"Everybody knows that," he insisted manfully. "It would be totally impracticable. Unfair on both of us."

She stared at him, her made-up lips apart and her eyes wide.

"I know it's hard," he said, touching the tip of her nose with his forefinger. She had a cute nose; he'd always liked it. "It's hard for both of us," he added, allowing himself a hint of reproach.

She carried on staring at him, and a frown was gathering between her eyebrows. She was obviously having trouble taking it in.

"It doesn't have to be right away," he insisted. "I think we should carry on as normal until the week or so before I leave. There's no need to break things up before then."

"What?" she said.

"Don't worry," he said. "You'll need time. We'll both need time. To adapt."

He took her shoulders and looked sorrowfully at her like a soldier in a film, off to the wars. He was going to be late for work. What came next? He lowered his face toward hers for a slow, pitying, notice-giving kiss.

That was when she went mad and started screaming and shouting and slapping out and ranting. In fact, she'd lost it. He'd had to grab his laptop and slam the door on her harpy act in the end and set off down Prince of Wales Drive at a brisk canter. Not his idea of a great start to the day. No cabs to be seen of course, and he was late, which didn't look good at the meeting, sidling in after everyone else. Not his style. But then, they knew that. Totally one-off.

It made for unease during the day, though. There was a lot on but even so his mind returned to the scene in the hall several times. He hadn't for a moment thought she'd get so hysterical about it. Surely she should be *pleased* for him. His mother was. Perhaps he shouldn't have told her until a couple of weeks before, but it had seemed only fair to give her as much notice as possible. *Too* fair, he thought wrathfully on his way to the sandwich bar. *Too* bloody fair, that was his trouble.

"Well done," said his colleagues. "When do you start?" And "What about Sarah?" asked one of them, Duncan Sharples, who'd come along for a glass of champagne at Windows on her birthday a few weeks ago.

"She knows the score," he replied. "Very much so. Obviously she got a bit emotional but she's got to be realistic like all of us have. It's modern life."

"So there'll be no prawns decomposing in the hollow curtain rail?" laughed Duncan. "No mustard and cress sprouting on the bedroom carpet?"

"Nothing like that," he said rather stiffly. "It's not even happening for another three months."

When he got back that night she was waiting in the hall, white in the face and red-eyed, ranting on immediately about coldness and insensitivity, emotional autism and more of her therapy crap.

"But there's no need to get like this now," he said, genuinely baffled. "We don't have to split up yet."

"Did you really think I'd carry on here eating with you and sleeping with you and doing all the girlfriend stuff, after . . . after . . ." And she started screaming at him again. He found that a real turnoff.

"I'm leaving tonight," she yelled at him. "I'll come and get the rest of my stuff later. When you're at work."

"But it's not for three months," he kept saying, flummoxed. She really didn't seem to understand.

"You are a total prat," she huffed. The doorbell rang. She went to the intercom.

"I'll be right down." She turned to him. "That's my cab."

"Sarah," he said, holding out his hands like a bad actor. "You don't have to go. You know that."

"PRAT," she spat and slammed the door behind her.

He felt a bit shaken by all this, despite himself. He did some shrugging, followed by one of his stress-buster breathing techniques. *Hoo-hoo-hoo,* he went; *hoo-hoo-hoo.* He had a quick check round the flat to see that she hadn't caused any damage. It was still in excellent decorative order, he noticed; he was sure he could rent it out no trouble. There was her photograph, the one of her laughing in a bikini last Christmas in St. Lucia. They'd had a really great time there, the hotel had been amazing. Had she forgotten all the good times? He wished he'd remembered to ask her that. He picked up the photograph and stared at her laughing face. It was a shock to think of its most recent expression, ashen and venomous. Quite unlike her. She was being incredibly—totally—unreasonable.

"Get off my case," he said, experimentally, at the photograph, and put it back facedown on top of the music center. He loaded a CD, turned up the volume for a blast of Arctic Monkeys.

Then he went into the kitchen and opened the fridge. He would obviously have to get his own zucchini-and-salmon bake tonight. She had gone completely over the top, he thought, as he stood waiting by the micro-wave. It pinged. For a moment he thought he was out-side the lift at work.

He donned the oven gloves and carefully removed the steaming box. The thing was, she was very young. He dug in with a fork. They both were really; but in the end she was immature with it. Whereas he wasn't. Quite the opposite. Fuck, it was hot. Which was why it was probably just as well. Now he'd burnt his *fucking* tongue. He ran a glass of cold water and stood there over the sink, shifting from foot to foot, swishing and spitting, swishing and spitting and swearing.

Scan

She was deep in London clay, a hundred feet underground, the train having paused for a rest just
short of Baker Street. In the darkness outside was vis-
ible the enfolding curve of the tunnel and also, at a
distance, a gleam of yellow, a worm with lampy eyes
making its way in another direction altogether. There
came into her mind wartime images of burrows and
shelters, the leaf-encircled entrance to a green lane;
landlocked landscapes with no sky or sea, no people
bar the odd melancholy dreamer like her reflection
in the window. The urge to hide was what powered
so many children's books of that time, escaping into
wardrobes or living under the floorboards; the Hob-
bit in his cozy bunker; midnight gardens silvered with

nostalgia, clocks transfixed so that time stood still. Since last week's diagnosis she had herself fallen out of time.

Perhaps this was what it was like, being born, the claustrophobic tunnel; you were being squeezed by the passage walls themselves, you were being pressed on centimeter by centimeter, with no inkling of the future but that far gleam of light. What about before you were born, though; before you were conceived? Well, you can't remember it so it can't have been too bad, she told herself; presumably it will be the same after you've died. The trouble with this idea was, before you've been born you've not been you; but once you've been alive you definitely *have* been you; and the idea of the extinction of the you that has definitely existed is quite different from the idea of your nonexistence before you did exist. Why were they stuck here? Had the train broken down?

She peered through the window and was able to make out thick cables running along the walls of the tunnel, regions of ribbed felty dust. When you're dead, surely you don't *know* you're dead. That would be too horrible. That would be a contradiction in terms. No, it would be like when you passed out; there was no memory of *that* afterward.

She'd started collapsing, blacking out, which was why she was now on her way for another test. "Let's take a look inside that head of yours." They wanted to see whether it had spread.

Now when she woke up in the morning the old unconscious happiness lasted only a few seconds before she remembered and thought, I wish this hadn't happened. But it had. There was an Anglo-Saxon word that meant "terror in the morning." *Morgencolla,* that was it: *morgencolla.* You'd wake just as it was getting light and see death coming up the river, the men with axes poised to leap out of their longboats and set fire to your home and disembowel you.

There came a whir, a whirring grumble, then a tense high-pitched hum and a rhythmic *chunk-a-chunk* vibration. Come on, she thought, come on or I'll be late. She glanced at her watch. There was a lurch, then nothing; another lurch, and they were inching toward the platform. It's all right, she thought once the doors had opened, it's all right, I'm not late yet, and she hurried with the others along tiled tunnels and up flights of sliding stairs.

Outside, on Baker Street, there were six lanes of traffic under a veil of fine-needled rain. A tall, beaky, sad-faced boy in a deerstalker and tweed cape from fifteen decades ago stood handing out leaflets to a general lack of interest. She took one and glanced at the sketch of Sherlock Holmes peering through his magnifying glass, the great detective on the trail of Moriarty. Past the shops selling bears in Beefeater outfits she hurried, past the tourists struggling with maps and collapsible umbrellas, then turned right at a church courtyard where cherry trees were loaded with sodden blossom, foolishly pink against the downcast sky. Another shortcut and she was into the windy wastes of Harley Street with its heavy one-way traffic. She checked the number of the place where she was to have this scan and saw how near it was. She wouldn't be late after all. A family dressed in full-length black stood weeping on its steps, their robes flapping in the wind. She averted her eyes and made her way inside.

Here, everybody was brightly lit, neutral and flat-faced. Thirty-four. Single. No children. Journalist. Yes, her employers provided private health insurance. MasterCard. The girl didn't look up once.

She paused at the mouth of the waiting room as if it were the entrance to the cave of suffering. Instinctively she knew about what went on in there, the long waits, disappointments, apparent improvements and the ugly reversals. She grabbed a magazine from the central table and stared at it. How to get the body you always wanted.

So it was her fault, then, what had happened. She hadn't been trying hard enough. In the absence of trouble she had imagined herself to be well, but now it seemed health was something that must be worked at, it must be courted with blueberries and pedometers and other expensive tokens of love. You had to be constantly on the qui vive for signs of betrayal or you were a fool. I thought I *was* my body, or at least friends with it, she observed; but obviously not. "No truly happy person grows a teratoma," said the Reiki healer she had consulted in her initial alarm. "Have you allowed yourself to be angry in your life?" *Angry?*

It was tempting to turn the blame inward, but that wouldn't do. Am I responsible for the filth in the air I breathe? she railed silently. Is the arrival of electrosmog my fault? My workplace is now an official Wi-Fi hotspot where we're all gently microwaving our internal organs, Bluetoothed radiation nibbling away at the blood-brain barrier. Maybe *that's* why I'm here, that bit further along the electromagnetic corridor, waiting for an exposure of my insides, and the promise of gamma rays next week. She was allowing herself to be angry now, certainly.

In the mirror of the changing cubicle her flesh looked denatured beneath the shadowless halogen light. Remove all jewelry. Once naked she realized she was still wearing her watch and unstrapped it. She was outside time now, along with the sick and the dead.

Last of all she shed her earrings, the starfish studs he had bought her in Brighton. Mr. X was how he was known at work—her new mystery man. She placed them carefully in one of her shoes. It was a definite farewell. She hadn't known him long enough to claim his company on such an unlooked for journey. "This has all been very sudden," she murmured, which was what you used to say when someone asked you to marry them. It wasn't just him, she hadn't told anybody yet; she needed to get used to the idea.

He might have enjoyed this unseemly hospital gown under other circumstances, open at the back, inadequately secured with ties. Never mind seeing her with no clothes on; she was about to be seen with no flesh on. The medical gaze was nothing if not penetrating.

They were after pictures of the inside of her imploding head. She lay down in the white gown on the motorized bed and inch by inch was drawn inside. The inexorable gliding pomposity of it reminded her of something, but she couldn't immediately think of what.

What was it? she wondered as she lay stiff and still in the viewless tunnel. Oh, of course, she thought as it came to her; it was the coffin's slow glide to curtains hiding the fire. This noise was very loud, the same as the walloping grumble and whine of the underground this morning but magnified tenfold. Someone had used the phrase "in case of claustrophobia" when they were explaining about the process, and now she realized why: the tunnel wall was six inches above her forehead.

So there would be twenty minutes of this, and she was still in the first. Her mind began leaping round all over the place. Keep calm. Think of something else. She'd been ignoring his texts and e-mails and the flashing Ansaphone. She felt pulled toward him but she must push him away; she couldn't face him but she wanted him. In her dream last night she'd been immune to traffic jams, high on a velvety camel swaying down St. Martin's Lane. It would be good if all *this* was just a dream, if in a little while she might wake up out of it, and stretch, and shrug it off.

It wouldn't work; she wouldn't be able to play at being a corpse for another eighteen minutes if she didn't get a grip. Time was getting stuck again, like the train in the tunnel. Time equals distance over speed. Time was supposed to slow down as it approached a black hole; the gravitational pull was so strong there that even light couldn't escape. A black hole was a star that had collapsed in on itself. She would have to harness her mind, put blinkers on, for the duration; otherwise she'd moan and groan and spoil the scan. Think of some careful time-consuming process, spin it out. Risotto, that would do.

She took an onion, hard and sound in its papery brown coat, and slit off its tight skin, sliced it in half. This loud grinding and thumping was like being deep in the bowels of a ship, down in the engine room with the men in boilersuits.

Narrowing her eyes against the tear-producing fumes, she cut the onion halves into fine layered crescents, then turned each half and diced the slices into lozenges. Think it through, she told herself, if you really can't stop thinking about what's happening. Magnetism is measured in gauss and tesla. Concentrate. Remember how it works. A fridge magnet has a pull of about 100 gauss, or 0.01 tesla. This machine has a magnetic field of 1 tesla, or 10,000 gauss.

Once she could smell the oil heating, she used the blade of the knife to send her diced onion over the edge of the chopping board and into the pan. There was a small sizzle and she turned the flame down. People would look uncomfortable or upset and say, Anything we can do, and treat her like a trip to the dentist.

So when the onions were soft and see-through, she'd add the rice. Flesh itself had become see-through thanks to the X-ray, whose discovery at the turn of the last century had whipped the press into a state of lubricious excitement. Not only could you see up her skirt, leered the papers, but with this machine you could now see *all the way.*

Push the enameled grains round with a wooden spoon, oiling them all over, introducing them to the onions. So here she was lying in a powerful magnetic field and next they would unloose a flood of high-frequency radio waves onto the scene. At this, all the water in her body—about 70 percent of her— would rise up. The hydrogen nuclei within her myriad water molecules would respond in a dance, aligning

themselves into patterns that a computer would trans-
form into images of whatever monster it was that was
crouching in there.

Add some stock, then wait until it's absorbed; add
some more and stir again. The tesla is the unit of magnetic flux density. The becquerel is the unit for mea-
suring radioactivity. Death is a camel that lies down at
every door. Watch it, it mustn't catch.

Surely it must be nearly over now. The noise was
getting louder. Don't be tempted to rush it. The noise
changed, the motorized bed started to move back-
ward, and she opened her eyes. She thought, My luck
has run out.

"All right there, are you?" said the nurse as she came
out of the tunnel.

"Fine," she smiled, breathing again, yawning, rubbing her face with her hands to revive the blood flow.
She couldn't wait to get away from the machinery and
the credit card swipe, the stale swagged grandeur of
the reception area.

Walking columns of water, she thought as she hurried down Weymouth Street. Even thought could be
photographed now, the synaptic spark in a rat's brain
like a jag of lightning. What happens to thought,
though, when the meat goes off?

She didn't have to go into work until after lunch
and it was still only eleven-fifty. A sub at work who
had needed chemotherapy last year had described how

she'd followed each session with a blast of retail therapy. Cheer herself up with a new lip gloss? Hardly. She bared her teeth then dialed his number on her mobile and waited, grimacing; heard the start of his voice message and cut the call straight off.

Behind the railings of the central garden in Manchester Square stood several large soot-eating plane trees just in leaf, bluebells brightening their roots. Where had her health gone? She went up to the railing spikes and took in some deep breaths, smelling the wet hawthorn on the other side. There she had been, taking it for granted, its good behavior and innocence; next thing she knew it was all over the place, it was in hysterics, threatening to leave her. Then it had packed its bags and walked out, slamming the door behind it.

Somewhere round here was an art collection, tucked away above the scrum of Oxford Street. "I'm sick of thinking about myself," she muttered. "I don't want to think about me." Here it was, at the top of the square, this red brick mansion—the Wallace Collection. She walked up to the swing doors. It was free.

Along the center of the entrance hall reared a marble staircase, winged snake-necked griffins biting its banisters. She went and stood over by the fireplace to one side of it. The clock on the mantelpiece was ticking in her ear. She checked the time it told against her watch, and it was right: twelve o'clock.

There came a silvery chiming from the room opposite, and distant carillons from other rooms too, the sound of midday chimes and striking mechanisms. I don't want to obey these rules, she thought, that everything's always going to be over and everyone must die.

She crossed into a room dominated by a massive freestanding chronometer on top of which lounged old Father Time, winged and bearded, and a baby holding a scythe. The clock itself, not content with mean time alone, also showed solar time, the passage of the sun through the zodiac, the age and phases of the moon, the date, the day of the week and the time at any place in the Northern Hemisphere. It was a skeleton clock: through the glass side panels you could see its elaborate working parts, the spring that must be wound once a month and the pendulum maintaining the regular beat.

This room was full of china in glass cabinets, soft paste Sèvres porcelain bulb pots and tea services in sea green, salmon pink and lapis blue. She took a laminated information sheet from the box by the door and started to read about cailloute and vermicule gilding, relishing the terminology of an unfamiliar technique where none of it remotely involved medical procedures. *Cailloute* meant pebblelike and *vermicule* was "worm tunnel." After the initial biscuit firing came the glazing process; then the paste was fired again and painted with cherubs or marine scenes or triple wreaths of foliage and flowers tied with ribbon. Last of all came the gilding. Honey and powdered gold had been brushed onto these vase brims and teacup handles three centuries ago, then fired, then burnished with a dog's tooth to increase the shine. A dog's tooth!

When they put art on a hospital wall it was to do with the need not to be reduced to a lump of gristle and malfunctioning cells. Here was Catherine the Great's ice cream cooler with a ground of bleu celeste. But a garage doesn't worry that it smells of oil and petrol; why *shouldn't* a hospital smell of surgery? They had not all been sent to the guillotine, as might have been expected; the Sèvres factory had carried on making porcelain, but with revolutionary symbols, Phrygian bonnets and tricolor flags instead of cherubs and roses.

She walked into a large gallery room and here he was again, in this little painting at eye level, the graybeard with his grizzled wings. At his feet was an infant holding up an hourglass. Time was just another name for death, she got the point. He was sitting to one side playing a lyre, providing the music for four beautiful heavy-limbed dancers who moved hand in hand in a ring and faced outward, fearless as children.

There are the facts of life, she thought, the predictable traps and horrors. What struck her now though was the irrelevance and centrality of emotion in human life and how the facts happened anyway, whatever you chose to feel about them.

Turning off into another room she was caught by

tender greens and blues and glimpses of amorous outdoor parties. *Le Petit Parc,* she read, *La Fête Galante.*
A girl in a loose lustring gown looked away, the nape
of her neck exposed to outdoor kisses, while her com-
panions lounged and whispered in each other's ears,
waiting for the lover who stood tuning his lute. In
the mid-distance a man looked out to sea through a
telescope.

Homesickness for the recent past brought savage
nausea. Garlands of fade-free flowers these paintings
promised; musical fountains and trees in perpetual
leaf. She wanted to climb up over the edges of their
frames, and clawed at the air. Her legs dissolved.

"Oh, I'm still here," she said, or tried to say, some minutes later. "I thought I was in a tunnel." Her view of
things was from a different angle. Just then the scene
above her whirled away as something else bulged
inside her head and burst.

Ahead of the Pack

Thank you for making the time to see me. I do appreciate how busy you are, so I'll talk fast! I'd like you to think of this presentation as a hundred-meter dash.

Yes, you're right, it can be difficult to find financing for a new idea. But not in this case. I'm far more concerned about someone stealing this idea than turning it down, to be honest; which is why I want to tie up a joint-venture agreement as soon as possible. By the end of the week, preferably.

So. A little bit about where I'm coming from first. My original background was in TEFL, then in PR for various NGOs—I've had something of a portfolio career—but in the last decade I have concentrated on developing my motivational skills in the areas of personal training and weight loss. I'm a zeitgeisty sort of person and I've found I have this unerring instinct for homing in on what the next big thing will be. You could say I'm like a canary in a mine shaft—but more positive, I hope!

The next big thing? Carbon dioxide is the next big thing! Yes, I am talking global warming, but please don't glaze over quite yet. Yes, I do know how boring it is, how much of a downer it can be but bear with me for the next seven minutes and I promise you'll be glad you did so.

I know, I know, there are still some people who say it isn't really happening, but they're like my weight-loss clients who say, "It's glandular" or "I've got big bones." What they're really saying is, they're not ready to change. Whereas the client who *is* ready to change is very often the one who's had a nasty scare. My prize dieter is a man who'd been living high for years and then a routine scan revealed completely furred-up carotid arteries. He had a great sense of humor, he used to wear a T-shirt with "I Ate All the Pies" on it, but underneath his heart was breaking. Literally. At two hundred and eighty pounds he was threatened with the very real prospect of a triple bypass, not to mention a double knee replacement, early-onset diabetes and gout.

Now, another client in a similar situation might have chosen to ignore the warning, opted to dig his grave with his own teeth, basically. I've seen that happen; I've been to the funeral. Fair enough, their choice. This man, though—a well-known local entrepreneur as it happens (no, I'm sorry, client confidentiality, I'm sure you'll understand)—this man directed his considerable drive toward losing ninety pounds over ten months, and as a matter of fact he finished in the first thirty-five thousand in this year's London Marathon.

And my point is? My point is, either we can carry on stuffing our faces and piling it on or we can decide to lose weight. We've suddenly acquired this huge communal spare tire of greenhouse gases; our bingeing has made the planet morbidly obese and breathless. Food, fuel; same difference. See where I'm coming from? And that was my eureka moment, when I realized that what's needed is a global weight-loss club.

I thought of calling it Team Hundred because we in the motivational world have a belief that it takes a hundred days to change a habit; plus, there are only a hundred months left in which to save the world, apparently. Then I tried Enough's Enough, but *that* was too strict, and possibly a teensy bit judgmental. Finally I came up with Ahead of the Pack, which I think you'll agree sounds both positive and urgent plus, it has the necessary lean competitive edge. Perfect!

It's simply a matter of time before it's compulsory for everyone, but those who've managed to adapt by choice, in advance, will be at a huge advantage. Ahead of the Pack! I mean, think of the difference between someone who's achieved gradual weight loss by adjusting their portion sizes and refusing second helpings and someone else who's wolfed down everything but the kitchen sink for years and years and then wonders why he needs gastric banding. I know which one I'd rather be.

Yes, you're right, that is exactly what I'm proposing—to set up as a personal carbon coach! In fact, I think you'll find that very soon it'll be mandatory for every company to employ an in-house emissions expert, so you might well find me useful here too in the not-too-distant future, if we're counting our chickens. The thing is, I have this program tailor-made and ready to rock. I've already test-driven it for free on several of my clients, and it's been fantastic.

First off I take their measurements, calculate the size of their carbon footprint—very like the BMI test, obviously, as carbon dioxide is measured in kilos too—and work out how far outside the healthy range they've strayed. We talk about why shortcuts don't work. Carbon sequestration and body-slimming apparel, for example, squash the bad stuff out of sight rather than make it disappear. And, somehow, magic solutions like fat-busting drugs and air scrubbers always seem to bring a nasty rash of side effects with them.

Anyway, we visit the fridge next, discuss the long-distance Braeburn apples and the antipodean leg of lamb, calculate their atmospheric calorie content. My clients generally pride themselves on their healthy eating habits, and they're amazed when I tell them that a flight from New Zealand is the equivalent of scarfing down two whole chocolate fudge cakes and an entire wheel of Brie. We move on, room by room, talking weight loss as we go, how to install loft insulation, where to find a local organic farm subscription; I give advice on fitting a water saver in the loo, and practical help with editing photo albums.

Photo albums? Oh yes. Very important.

In ten years' time, we'll be casting round for scapegoats. Children will be accusing parents, and wise parents will have disappeared all visual evidence of Dad's gap year in South America and Mum on Ayers Rock and the whole gang over in Florida waiting in line to shake Mickey's hand. Junk your fatso habits now, I advise them, get ahead of the pack, or you'll find yourself exposed—as hypocritical as a Victorian adjusting his antimacassars while the sweep's boy chokes to death up the chimney. Nobody will be able to plead ignorance, either. We can all see what's happening, on a daily basis, on television.

And if they have a second home I advise them to sell it immediately—sooner, if the second home is abroad. Of course! Instant coronary time! Talk about a hot potato.

Really? Oh. Oh.

I hear what you're saying. You think I'm going directly against my target client base with that advice. Yes. Well, maybe I do need to do some tweaking, some fine-tuning.

Basically though, and I'm aware that I've had my ten minutes, and I'd like to take this opportunity to thank you for your time—basically, is it your feeling that you're prepared to invest in Ahead of the Pack?

You'll get back to me on that one. I see. I see.

So, you happen to have a house near Perpignan, do you? Yes, it certainly is your hard-earned money. A bit of a wreck but if you can get there for £29, why shouldn't you? No reason, no reason. O reason not the need, as Shakespeare says! As long as you know of course it means that, globally speaking, in terms of your planetary profile, you've got an absolutely vast arse.

Sorry?

"Sorry?" said Patrick. "I didn't quite catch that."

"SOUP OF THE DAY IS WILD MUSH-ROOM," bellowed the waiter.

"No need to shout," said Patrick, putting his hand to his troublesome ear.

The new gadget screeched in protest.

"They take a bit of getting used to," grimaced Matthew Herring, the deaf chap he'd been fixed up with for a morale-boosting lunch.

"You don't say," he replied.

Some weeks ago Patrick had woken up to find he had gone deaf in his right ear—not just a bit deaf but profoundly deaf. There was nothing to be done, it

62 ·

seemed. It had probably been caused by a tiny flake of matter dislodged by wear-and-tear change in the vertebrae, the doctor had said, shrugging. He had turned his head on his pillow, in all likelihood; sometimes that was all it took. This neck movement would have shifted a minuscule scrap of detritus into the river of blood running toward the brain, a fragment that must have finished by blocking the very narrowest bit of the entire arterial system, the ultrafine pipe leading to the inner ear. Bad luck.

"I don't hear perfectly," said Matthew Herring now. "It's not magic, a digital hearing aid, it doesn't turn your hearing into perfect hearing."

"Mine's not working properly yet," said Patrick. "I've got an appointment after lunch to get it seen to."

"Mind you, it's better than the old one," continued Matthew comfortably. "You used to be able to hear me wherever I went with the analog one—it used to go before me, screeching like a steam train."

He chuckled at the memory.

Patrick did not smile at this cozy reference to engine whistles. He had been astonished at the storm of head noise that had arrived with deafness, the whistles and screeches over a powerful cloud of hissing just like the noise from his wife Elizabeth's old pressure cooker. His brain was generating sound to compensate for the loss of hearing, he had been told. Apparently that was part and parcel of the deafness, as well as dizzy episodes. Ha! Thanks to the vertigo that had sent him arse over tip several times since the start of all this, he was having to stay with his daughter Rachel for a while.

"Two girls," he said tersely in answer to a question from his tedious lunch companion. He and Elizabeth had wished for boys, but there you were. Rachel was the only one so far to have provided him with grandchildren. The other daughter, Ruth, had decamped to Australia some time ago. Who knew what she was up to but she was still out there so presumably she had managed to make a go of it, something she had signally failed to do in England.

"I used to love music," Matthew Herring was saying, undaunted. "But it's not the same now that I'm so deaf. Now it tires me out; in fact, I don't listen anymore. I deliberately avoid it. The loss of it is a grief, I must admit."

"Oh well, music means nothing to me," said Patrick. "Never has. So I shan't miss *that*."

He wasn't about to confide in Matthew Herring, but of all his symptoms it had been the auditory hallucinations produced by the hearing aid that had been the most disturbing for him. The low violent stream of nonsense issuing from the general direction of his firstborn had become insupportable in the last week, and he had had to turn the damned thing off.

· · ·

At his after-lunch appointment with the audiologist, he found himself curiously unable to describe the hallucinatory problem.

"I seem to be picking up extra noise," he said eventually. "It's difficult to describe."

"Sounds go into your hearing aid, where they are processed electronically," she intoned, "then played back to you over a tiny loudspeaker."

"Yes, I know that," he snapped. "I am aware of that, thank you. What I'm asking is, might one of the various settings you programmed be capable of, er, amplifying sounds that would normally remain unheard?"

"Let's see, shall we," she said, still talking to him as though he were a child or a half-wit. "I wonder whether you've been picking up extra stuff on the Loop."

"The Loop?"

"It works a bit like Wi-Fi," she said. "Electromagnetic fields. If you're in an area that's on the Loop, you can pick up on it with your hearing aid when you turn on the T-setting."

"The T-setting?"

"That little extra bit of doohickey there," she said, pointing at it. "I didn't mention it before; I didn't want to confuse you while you were getting used to the basics. You must have turned it on by mistake, from what you're saying."

"But what *sort* of extra sounds does it pick up?" he persisted.

Rachel's lips had not been moving during that initial weird diatribe a week ago, he was sure of it, nor during the battery of bitter little remarks he'd had to endure since then.

"Well, it can be quite embarrassing," the audiologist said, laughing merrily. "Walls don't block the magnetic waves from a Loop signal, so you might well be able to listen in on confidential conversations if neighboring rooms are also on it."

"Hmm," he said, "I'm not sure that quite explains this particular problem. But I suppose it might have something to do with it."

"Look, I've turned off the T-setting," she said. "If you want to test what it does, simply turn it on again and see what happens."

"Or hear," he said. "Hear what happens."

"You're right!" she declared, with more merry laughter.

He really couldn't see what was so amusing, and said so.

Back at Rachel's, he made his way to the armchair in the little bay window and whiled away the minutes until six o'clock by rereading the *Telegraph*. The trouble with this house was that its interior walls had been knocked down, so you were all in it hugger-mugger together. He could not himself see the advantage of being forced to witness every domestic detail. Frankly, it was bedlam, with the spin cycle going and Rachel's twins screeching and Rachel washing her hands at the kitchen sink yet again like Lady Macbeth. Now she was doing that thing she did with the brown paper bag, blowing into it and goggling her eyes, which seemed to amuse the twins at least.

Small children were undoubtedly tiresome, but the way she indulged hers made them ten times worse. Like so many of her generation she seemed to be making a huge song and dance about the whole business. She was ridiculous with them, ludicrously overindulgent and lacking in any sort of authority. It was when he had commented on this in passing that the auditory hallucinations had begun.

"I don't want to do to them what you did to me, you old beast," the voice had growled, guttural and shocking, although her lips had not been moving. "I don't want to hand on the misery, I don't want that horrible Larkin poem to be true." He had glared at her, amazed, and yet it had been quite obvious that she was blissfully unaware of what he had heard. Or thought he had heard.

He must have been hearing things.

Now he held up his wrist and tapped his watch at her. She waved back at him, giving one last puff into the paper bag before scurrying to the fridge for the ice and lemon. As he watched her prepare his first drink of the evening, he decided to test out the audiologist's theory.

"Sit with me," he ordered, taking the clinking glass.

"I'd love to, Dad, but the twins . . . ," she said.

"Nonsense," he said. "Look at them, you can see them from here—they're all right for now."

She perched on the arm of the chair opposite his and started twisting a strand of her lank brown hair.

"Tell me about your day," he commanded.

"My day?" she said. "Are you sure? Nothing very much happened. I took the twins to playgroup, then we went round the supermarket."

"Keep talking," he said, fiddling with his hearing aid. "I want to test this gadget out."

". . . then I had to stand in line at the post office, and I wasn't very popular with the double stroller," she droned on.

He flicked the switch to the T-setting.

". . . never good enough for you, you old beast, you never had any time for me, you never listened to anything I said," came the low growling voice he remembered from before. "You cold old beast, Ruth says you're emotionally autistic, definitely somewhere on the autistic spectrum anyway, that's why she went to the other side of the world but she says she still can't get away from it there, your lack of interest, you blanked us, you blotted us out, you don't even know

the names of your grandchildren let alone their birth-
days . . ."

He flicked the switch back.

". . . after their nap, then I put the washing on
and peeled some potatoes for tonight's dinner while
they watched CBeebies," she continued in her toneless
everyday voice.

"That's enough for now, thanks," he said crisply. He
took a big gulp of his drink, and then another. "Scar-
lett and, er, Mia. You'd better see what they're up to."

"Are you OK, Dad?"

"Fine," he snapped. "You go off and do whatever it
is you want to do." He closed his eyes. He needed Elizabeth now. She'd taken no nonsense from the girls. He
had left them to her, which was the way she'd wanted
it. All this hysteria! Elizabeth had known how to deal
with them.

He sensed he was in for another bad night, and he
was right. He lay rigid as a stone knight on a tomb,
claustrophobic in his partially closed-down head and
its frantic brain noise. The deafer he got, the louder it
became; that was how it was, that was the deal. He
grimaced at the future, his other ear gone, reduced to
the company of Matthew Herring and his like, a shoal
of old boys mouthing at each other.

The thing was, he had been the breadwinner. Children needed their mothers. It was true he hadn't been

very interested in them, but then, frankly, they hadn't been very interesting. Was he supposed to pretend? Neither of them had amounted to much. And, he had had his own life to get on with.

He'd seen the way they were with their children these days—"Oh that's wonderful darling! You *are* clever" and "Love you!" at the end of every exchange, with the young fathers behaving like old women, cooing and planting big sloppy kisses on their babies as if they were in a Disney film. The whole culture had gone soft, it gave him the creeps; opening up to your feminine side! He shuddered in his pajamas.

Elizabeth was dead. That was what he really couldn't bear.

The noise inside his head was going wild, crackles and screeching and pressure-cooker hisses; he needed to distract his brain with—what had the doctor called it?—"sound enrichment." Give it some competition, fight fire with fire; that was the idea. Fiddling with the radio's tuning wheel in the dark, he swore viciously and wondered why it was you could never find the World Service when you needed it. He wanted talk but there was only music, which would have to do. Nothing but a meaningless racket to him, though at least it was a different *sort* of racket; that was the theory.

No, that was no better. If anything, it was worse.

Wasn't the hearing aid supposed to help cancel tinnitus? So the doctor had suggested. Maybe the

T-setting would come into its own in this sort of situation. He turned on the tiny gadget, made the necessary adjustments, and poked it into his ear.

It was like blood returning to a dead leg, but in his head and chest. What an extraordinary sensation! It was completely new to him. Music was stealing hotly, pleasurably through his veins for the first time in his life, unspeakably delicious. He heard himself moan aloud. The waves of sound were announcing bliss and at the same time they brought cruel pain. He'd done his best, hadn't he? He didn't know what the girls expected from him. He'd given them full financial support until they were eighteen, which was more than many fathers could say. What was it exactly that he was supposed not to have done?

Lifting him on a dark upsurge into the night, the music also felled him with inklings of what he did not know and had not known, intimations of things lovely beyond imagination which would never now be his as death was next. A tear crept down his face.

He hadn't cried since he was a baby. Appalling! At this rate he'd be wetting himself. When his mother had died, he and his sisters had been called into the front room and given a handkerchief each and told to go to their bedrooms until teatime. Under the carpet. Into thin air.

The music was so astonishingly beautiful, that was the trouble. Waves of entrancing sound were threatening to breach the sea wall. Now he was coughing dry sobs.

This was not on. Frankly, he preferred any combination of troublesome symptoms to getting in this state. He fumbled with the hearing aid and at last managed to turn the damned thing *off.* Half-unhinged, he tottered to the bathroom and ran a basin of water over it, submerged the beastly little gadget, drowned it. Then he fished it out and flushed it down the lavatory. Best place for it.

No more funny business, he vowed. That was that. From now on he would put up and shut up, he swore it on Elizabeth's grave. Back in bed, he once again lowered his head onto the pillow.

Straightaway the infernal noise factory started up; he was staggering along beat by beat in a heavy shower of noise and howling.

"It's not real," he whispered to himself in the dark. "Compensatory brain activity, that's what this is."

Inside his skull all hell had broken loose. He had never heard anything like it.

The Tipping Point

L ook at that sky. It's almost sitting on the windshield. Whose idea was it to hold Summer School
up in the wilds this year? I know my sweet Americans would follow me to the ends of the earth for my
thoughts on the Bard; and I know Stratford venues are
stratospheric these days. But all this way to study the
Scottish play in situ smacks of desperation. If ever a
sky looked daggers, this is it.

I was quite looking forward to the drive, actually. Impossible to get lost, my esteemed colleague
Malkie MacNeil told me; just follow the A82 all the
way and enjoy the scenery, the mountains, best in the
world, blah blah. So I left Glasgow reasonably bright
and hopeful this morning after a dish of porridge,

up along Loch Lomond, and the light has drained steadily away through Tarbet, Ardlui, Tyndrum, until I realize that it's eleven in the morning on the fifth of August and I've got to turn on the headlights. Storm clouds over Glencoe. "The cloud-capp'd Towers, the gorgeous Palaces." Not really. More like a celestial housing estate.

All right, let's have something suitably gloomy in the way of music. Here we are. *Winterreise* with Dietrich Fischer-Dieskau and his manly baritone. No finer example of the pathetic fallacy than Schubert's *Winterreise*. "What's that when it's at home, Dr. Beauman?" That is the reading of one's own emotion into external nature, child. I still cannot believe that I, confirmed commitmentphobe, have been cast as the rejected lover, ignominiously dumped like some soppy freshman.

Nun ist die Welt so trübe, / Der Weg gehült in Schnee. My German may not be fluent but it's become more than passable in the last year. You'd allow that, Angelika? Now the world is so bleak, the path shrouded in snow. *Schnee.*

It was immediate. As soon as we first clapped eyes on each other, et cetera. But, joking apart, it was. I was over in Munich to give my paper "Milton's *Comus*; the Masque Form as Debate and Celebration," mainly because I wanted to check out the painted rococo Cuvilliés-Theater—crimson, ivory and gold—on Residenzstrasse. I needed it for my chapter on European court theater, for the book that now bears your name as dedicatee.

You were in charge of that conference, head of arts admin for all the participating institutions that week. Once it was over we went back to your flat in Cologne. Jens was staying with his grandmother as luck would have it. Beautiful Angelika, with your fierce pale eagle eyes and beaming smile. I remember capering round your bed like a satyr after you'd given me the first of your ecological curtain lectures. I was quoting *Comus* at you to shut you up:

> *Wherefore did Nature pour her bounties forth*
> *With such a full and unwithdrawing hand,*
> *Covering the earth with odours, fruits, and flocks,*
> *Thronging the seas with spawn innumerable,*
> *But all to please and sate the curious taste?*

I was proud and stout and gleeful in the presence of your angularity. It felt like a challenge. Heaping you with good things became part of that. I filled your austere kitchen with delicacies, though that wasn't easy as you are of course vegan.

"Enough is enough," you said, pushing me away.

"You can never have enough," I laughed. "Didn't you know that?"

"Not so. I have."

Ich will den Boden küssen, / Durchdringen Eis und

Schnee / Mit meinen heissen Tränen. Schnee again. I want to kiss the ground, to pierce the ice and snow with my hot tears. Yes, well. Romanticism was your besetting sin, Angelika; your quasi-mystical accusatory ecospeak about the planet. Whereas my line is, if it's going to happen, it's going to happen—I don't see how anything mankind does can impose change on overwhelming natural phenomena like hurricanes and tsunamis. We resemble those frail figures in a painting by Caspar David Friedrich, dwarfed by the immensity of nature. You took me to see his great painting *Das Eismeer* in the Hamburger Kunsthalle, jagged ice floes in a seascape beyond hope; and you used it as a jumping-off point to harangue me about the collapse of the Larsen B Ice Shelf. My clever intense passionate Angelika, so quick to imagine the worst, and so capable of anguish; you wept like a red-eyed banshee when you gave me the push.

An ominous cloudscape, this, great weightless barricades of cumulonimbus blocking the light. I can't see another car or any sign of humanity. Once out of this miserable valley, I'll stop for gas in Ballachulish. Then it's on up past Loch Linnhe, Loch Lochy, Loch Oich, Loch Ness, and I'll be there. Inverness. What's done is done. Halfway through the week there's a day trip planned to Cawdor Castle, where Duncan doubtless shakes his gory locks on mugs and mouse pads all over the gift shop.

So then I applied for a peripatetic fellowship at the University of Cologne and got it. I brushed up my Schiller. I wrote a well-received paper on Gotthold Lessing's *Minna von Barnhelm* and gave a seminar on Ödön von Horváth, the wandering playwright who all his life was terrified of being struck by lightning and then, during a Parisian thunderstorm, took shelter beneath a tree on the Champs-Élysées and was killed by a falling branch. Let that be a warning to you, Angelika: you can worry too much.

We were very happy, you and me and Jens. He's unusually thoughtful and scrupulous, that boy; like his mother. They had their annual day of atonement at his school while I was over, when the children are instructed to consider the guilt of their militaristic forefathers in the last century. That was the night he had an asthma attack and we ended up in casualty. Cue copious lectures from you on air quality, of course.

And here's the rain, driving against the windshield with a violence fit to crack it. It's almost comic, this journey, the menace of those massed clouds, the gray-green gloom. Nor do I have a residual belief that rain is in any way cleansing or purgative. No, no. As you so painstakingly taught me, Angelika, our sins of pollution lock into the clouds and come down as acid rain. Hence *Waldsterben,* or forest death; and from *Waldsterben* you would effortlessly segue into flash floods, storm surge, wildfire, drought, and on to carbon sequestration. You were not the only one. You and your friends discussed these things for hours, drawing up petitions, marching here and there. Your activism made my English students look like solipsistic children, their political concerns stretching with some effort to tuition fees and back down again to the price of hair straighteners.

You were in a constant state of alarm. I wanted you to talk about me, about you and me, but the apocalyptic zeitgeist intruded.

Darling, shall we go for a swim? No, my love, for the oceans have warmed up and turned acidic. All plankton is doomed and, by association, all fish and other swimmers. Sweetheart, what can I do to melt your heart? Nothing, for you are indifferent to the ice-albedo feedback; you are unconcerned that the planet's shield of snow, which reflects heat back into space, is defrosting. That our world grows dangerously green and brown, absorbing more heat than ever before, leaves you cold.

My own dear heart, let's make a happy future for ourselves, for you and me and Jens. How can that be when the world is melting and you don't care? How can we be *gemütlich* together in the knowledge that the twin poles of the world are dissolving, that permafrost is no longer permanent and will unloose vast clouds of methane gas to extinguish us all?

You did love me. You told me so. *Ich liebe Dich.*

Then came your ultimatum. We couldn't go on seeing each other like this. Yes, you loved my flying vis-
its, you loved being with me. But no, you could not
bear it that our love was sustained at the expense of
the future. By making it dependent on cut-rate flights
we were doing the single worst possible thing in our
power as private individuals to harm the planet.

"Love miles," I countered, morally righteous, fighting fire with fire.

"Selfish miles," you retorted. "We are destroying
other people's lives when we do this." Very truthful
and severe you are, Angelika; very hard on yourself as
well as others.

Time for a change of CD. More Schubert lieder,
I think, but let's drop Fischer-Dieskau. He's a tad
heavyhearted for Scotland, a bit of a dampener where
it's already damp enough. Ah, Gérard Souzay, he's my
man. Rather an eccentric choice, but my father used to
listen to him and I cottoned on to what he admired. A
great voice, fresh, rich, essentially baritonal but keener
on beauty than usual. Let's skip "Der Jüngling und der
Tod," though. OK, here comes the Erl King. There's a
boy here, too, riding on horseback through the night
with his father, holding close to his father. Oh, it's
a brilliant micro-opera, this song, one voice singing
four parts—narrator, father, boy and the lethal whee-
dling Erl King. I'd forgotten how boldly elliptical it
is, and how infectious the boy's terror—*"Mein Vater,*

mein Vater, und hörest du nicht, / Was Erlenkönig mir leise versprichtं?" My father, my father, and don't you hear / the Erl King whispering promises to me? But his father can't hear anything, can't see anything, only the wind and the trees.

I used to start laughing uncontrollably at this point, which annoyed *my* father, who was trying to listen; but it appealed to my puerile sense of humor—*Vater* as "farter."

Mein Vater, mein Vater, jetzt fasst er mich an!
Erlkönig hat mir ein Leids getan!

My father, my father, now he is taking hold of me! / The Erl King has hurt me! And by the time the father has reached home the boy lies dead in his arms. *Tot.*

Listen, Angelika. You make my blood boil. What possible difference can it make whether I get on a plane or not? The plane will take off regardless. Why don't you concentrate your energies on all those herds of farting cattle, eh? All those cows and sheep farting and belching. Then after that you could get the rain forests under control! The blazing forests! You don't want me.

It's stopped raining at last. I can see ahead again, the air is clearer now. A truly theatrical spectacle, this sky, with its constant changes of scene. I couldn't do it in the end. I wanted tenure, sure, but I was being asked to give up too much. The world. The world well lost? No. No, no, not even for you, Angelika.

In September I'm attending a weekend conference on performance art at the Uppsala University, in Sweden. I'm not going by bus. There's a seminar on *Sturm und Drang* in Tokyo this autumn, as well as my Cardiff-based sister's wedding party in Seville. After that there's an invitation to the Sydney Festival to promote my new book, and the usual theater conference at Berkeley in the spring. All paid for, of course, except the return ticket to Seville, which cost me precisely £11—just about manageable even on an academic's meager stipend.

You used to have to join the Foreign Office if you wanted to travel on anything like this scale. Now everybody's at it. The budget airlines arrived and life changed overnight. Sorry, but it's true. The world's our sweetshop. We've got used to it, we want it; there's no going back.

The downside is, I lost my love. She followed through. And how. She caused us both enormous pain. Ah, come on! For all I know, she's gotten back together with that little dramaturg from Bremen, the one with the tiny hands and feet. So?

Look at those schmaltzy sunbeams backlighting the big gray cloud. Perfect scenery for the arrival of a deus ex machina. "What's that when it's at home, Dr. Beau-man?" A far-fetched plot device to make everything all right again, my dear. There's Ballachulish in the distance. A painted god in a cardboard chariot. An unlikely happy ending, in other words.

Geography Boy

They were up very early against the heat, panniers packed and off on their bikes toward Angers before anybody else at the youth hostel was awake. It felt like the beginning of the world, with the fresh damp smell of the hedgerows and the faint reveille from a rooster several fields away, although it was in fact the last day of their holiday. Six weeks ago they had met at a party, in the summer term of their second year. Neither of them had ever felt this strongly before about anyone.

Adele was majoring in History and had chosen the End of the World module rather than the History of Human Rights as her latest term paper topic. It was because of this that she had suggested adding Angers to their itinerary, after reading the guidebook's rapt account of the apocalyptic tapestries there.

"It's the largest wall hanging ever to be woven in Europe," she had quoted from the guidebook the other night in Chinon. "Six huge tapestry panels, each with fourteen scenes displayed on two levels, like a sort of double-decker cartoon full of monsters and catastrophes."

"Can't wait," Brendan had said chivalrously. His subject was geography, and he was aware that he had probably dragged her round one too many troglodyte caves that day. Amazing, though, the way those caves had been created by chance from quarrying for the local tufa limestone with which to build the white châteaux of the Loire. The damp ones were now used for mushroom cultivation, their guide had informed them, while the rest were being lived in or snapped up by Parisians as *résidences secondaires.* "I'd like to live in a cave with you," he had wanted to say to Adele, but hadn't been quite brave enough.

They were bowling along between fields of ripe corn, and he felt like singing or shouting. Sometimes in the last week, when they had been swooping down a hill in the forests near Chinon, he had shouted aloud into the air rushing past him in sheer exhilaration. Then there was the long stiff climb up the next one, moving the piston legs, ignoring the keen sensation in the front thigh muscles of being flooded with boiling water, Adele panting alongside him, and the reward at the top, as their hearts gradually stopped pounding and they gloated once again over the sweet swooping downward stretch ahead.

On they cycled as the sun climbed higher and the day grew hotter. Sweat was flying from their faces now, and inside their clothes it was trickling down their bodies as they pistoned forward. There were few cars—perhaps one every ten minutes or so—although evidence of their existence was displayed at intervals along the way, flattened hedgehogs, little birds and mice. Once, by a low orchard of strictly serried apple trees, there had been a great silver serpent, half a meter long, flattened in mid-zigzag.

"Château," he called as they rounded a bend in the road. There it was, white against the green, another one, the twenty-seventh this holiday, set in an illuminated meadow of grass and flowers with the shining river beyond. These châteaux were like the ones in fairy tales, she had said earlier in the holiday, the sort where Sleeping Beauty might be found. You're my sleeping beauty, he had told her, but she had rejected that particular princess as a bad role model—too passive—and had told him it was Little Red Riding Hood who was now recommended to girls, for her ingenuity and resourcefulness. He had tried to make her promise to join him in his activism next term; it's no longer a case of crying wolf, he'd told her; the end of the world really is nigh. Too late, she had replied; it's too late.

"Money's won," she'd said with a shrug. "It's obvious."

"But the worst thing we can do now is nothing," he'd cried.

At this she had shrugged again and returned to her book.

"Baguette stop?" he called to her now after an hour or so on the road. The sun was already strong in a bold blue sky sparsely plumed with cirrus clouds.

"D'accord."

They set their bikes against a wall at the edge of a field of sunflowers, in the shade of one of a line of whispering silver-green poplars planted three generations ago. There were armies of these sunflowers round here, great thick stalks as tall as a man, dinner-plate faces turning heavily in the direction of the sun. The thing was, Brendan had faith in the world's adaptive powers, whereas Adele didn't, it seemed.

While he unstrapped the water bottles, she took out some bread and fruit saved from the night before. She started to clean the peaches by rubbing off their down with the hem of her T-shirt, then paused to watch as he drank, his head flung back, his eyes closed.

"Last day," he scowled, wiping his mouth with the back of his hand. "I wish it wasn't."

"Can you remember all the days in order? Where was it we cycled first, after Tours?"

She went up and wound her arms round his damp waist, inhaling his heat and the grassy smell of sweat drying.

"It was that Plantagenet place, the abbey with the painted king and queen on top of their tombs," he said, tucking her head beneath his chin. "Fontevraud. The queen was Eleanor of Aquitaine."

"Yes. And their son was on his tomb beside them, Richard the Lionheart. Remember? The Crusades. Crushing the infidel."

"I'll crush you," he said foolishly, twisting her arms behind her back.

She was pressed close to his chest, her ear against the thump of his heart.

They were testing each other on this holiday, competitive and protective and teasing. It was neck and neck so far. She didn't yet know if she had met her match. Sometimes she suspected not, and this made her feel like crying. Anyway, how can we promise to stay together when we don't know how we'll change? thought Adele. Look at my parents. Look at anyone. Brendan was thinking, I want her in my bed and at my side now and for good. We belong together; it's a fact, not a choice.

She pulled away and started to eat a peach.

"You've got juice on your chin," he said, watching as she ate.

"No!" she flared at him even before he finished speaking, laughing.

"No what?"

"Just no."

"How did you know what I was going to say?"

"It's too hot," she said, blushing.

He pulled himself up to sit on the wall where the bicycles rested; with a broad smile he held his arms out to her.

He had begun to look fierce and brick-brown with sun damage, she thought, like some sort of wild man or wandering minstrel. One evening she had told him what she knew about troubadours and courtly love in the Middle Ages, about their songs and code of courtesy and chivalric belief that desire was in itself ennobling; all that. He had listened intently before seizing an imaginary lute and capering to and fro and warbling rubbish, until she, cracked into unwilling laughter, had run about trying to swat him as he dodged and skipped round her.

"It's what the French call *bronzer idiot*," she said now, rubbing a fingerful of sunscreen into his forehead, his cheeks, his chin and neck. He took her hand and turned it, kissing inside the wrist, then pulled her round so that she was leaning back, an elbow on each of his knees. He undid the clip holding up her sweat-damp hair and twisted it slowly, held it away from her head.

"No wonder you're so hot with all this hair," he murmured. "Hothead."

She closed her eyes, ensnared by thoughts of the night before.

"We're making good time," said Brendan after a while, glancing at his watch and at the sky. "We'll be there soon after midday at this rate."

Once at Angers, they found a shady patch of grass by the Maine, beneath the château, where they could lie and eat their *supermarché* picnic. They had bought cherries, a small soot-coated goat's cheese and some cold beer.

"It's not one of the fairy-tale ones, is it," said Adele, looking up at the massive, black-striped circular towers.

"More of a fortress than a château," said Brendan, following her gaze and taking a swig of beer. He rolled the bottle over his brow and then along the inside of her arm.

"Angers, city of Cointreau. Château built between 1229 and 1240. Famous for Apocalypse tapestries," said Adele, frowning over the guidebook. "They say famous, but I've never heard of them. Not like the Bayeux tapestry. Do you want to know what it says about them?"

"In a nutshell," said Brendan. He was rifling through the bag of cherries.

"Oof, let's see. In a nutshell. Well, they were commissioned by the Duke of Anjou, not long after the Black Death. He used them to show off, bringing them out for jousts and troubadour events and that sort of thing. Then they were given to Angers cathedral, which had trouble displaying them because they were so enormous."

He smoothed her hair back gently and hung twin cherries over her ears.

"Look, I've made you earrings!"

"Thank you. Then came the French Revolution and religion was out the window. Bits of the tapestries were chopped off and used for rubbing down horses, or as bed canopies, or to clear up after building work."

"Would you pass me another beer?"

"Won't you be too sleepy then to go round the château?"

"I'll be fine," he said. "Weird to think of the French as revolutionaries. They take their cats for walks on leashes! Remember that woman in Saumur?"

"Then in the nineteenth century there was a craze on the Middle Ages," she continued. "They rescued the tapestries and washed them in the Maine, which did their plant-based pigments no good at all. That's why the trees and grass are blue. And in the twentieth century they restored them and built a special long gallery in the château grounds to house them."

"Do you know, your ears are perfect. Very rare, perfect ears," murmured Brendan. "Come here, we need a siesta."

Adele lay in the crook of his arm with her head on his shoulder.

"You look like that king on his tomb in Fontevraud," she murmured to his profile. "Calm and complete."

"You're my queen," he breathed, before falling asleep. She lay moving gently to the rise and fall of his chest.

They were in a long dimly lit gallery and had the place almost to themselves. As they dawdled along, every now and then one of them would hold the other back to examine a detail, the grapy clusters of a cloud or the leaf-shaped flames of hell.

"The guidebook was right: see, all the grass and trees and foliage are blue," said Brendan. "Look at the shapes of the leaves! That's an oak, that's a vine leaf. Look at the detail."

"And these must be the Four Horsemen of the Apocalypse," said Adele. "Yes, see, there's Famine on that black horse there. And look, look at this skeleton grinning as he trots past the blue jaws of hell—that's Death on his pale horse."

"Nice," said Brendan, peering at the fine-stitched skull.

"Look! Seven angels with seven trumpets, heralding seven different disasters, just like in Revelations."

"Revelations?"

"It's the book that got tacked on to the end of the New Testament. It nearly didn't get in at all. It's raving. I had to read it for my special topic last term, remember?"

"Oh, yes. The End of the World. Of course."

"Full of stuff about the Whore of Babylon and the Antichrist and seven-headed monsters," she sniffed. "Seven was supposed to be some sort of magic number. Apocalyptic talk always comes from nutters, and they always quote Revelations. It's like a rule. Basically, they want a purge, a wipeout. They justify it with the Bible, then they say everything afterward will be purified and perfect for the survivors. Nee-naw nee-naw."

"I want you on board next term, Adele. You've got to join my protest group. There's no way you're going to get out of it."

"Oh, not that again, Brendan."

"Sorry," he said, hurt.

"No, I'm sorry," she said and gently butted her forehead against his arm.

There was a pause.

"So," he continued, almost reluctantly, "so, up till

now everyone involved in any of this end-of-the-world stuff has been raving mad and nothing but trouble. That's what you're saying. But now, now that it really does look like it's about to be all over, we can't seem to get a grip at all. Is that it?"

"If you like," she sighed.

"Kiss me."

She paused and did as he asked, slowly, thoughtfully, then took a step away from him.

"Come on," she said, taking his hand and pulling him along to the next panel. "It's a big tapestry. Look at this shipwreck, it's amazing. See, the floods have come. Look at the faces on the drowning men—their mouths are open, you can see their little teeth."

"Floods! I could use this next term. I wonder if they've got a postcard of it. It's brilliant! Sorry. Sorry. But you're right; look at the expressions on those faces!"

"I suppose I did rather cover the same material," she said, relenting for a moment. "Floods, drought, storms, all that. 'The Environment, Human Activity and the End of the World.' Only two of us chose it; they nearly didn't run it. The module on human rights was way more popular."

"That's what pisses me off about students," declared Brendan. "So fucking shortsighted. We want to travel, basically."

"Give it a rest, Brendan!" she said, losing her temper. "Can't we talk about something else?"

She marched on ahead of him. He stood and ground his teeth and took a deep breath.

No, he wanted to say, no we bloody well can't; you've got to listen to me; you don't get it, do you. He swallowed his exasperation and made an effort to do as she'd asked.

"That's the star Wormwood," she said when he caught up with her at the next panel.

"I thought wormwood was some sort of bitter plant," he said curtly.

"It's a star that streams blood," she read from the guidebook, "and pollutes the skies and oceans."

"Wormwood," muttered Brendan, drawn in despite himself. "Wow."

"Moving on past the Eagle of Misfortune, we get to the locusts swarming up from hell. Ha. They're enormous. They really are quite scary."

"Locusts! The insects are winning. You won't be so cocky when we've all got malaria."

"Brendan."

"It's all right for the middle-aged ones, the ones in charge now," he burst out, unable to contain himself. "But they're deliberately not looking into the time when it'll be our turn. Because by that time they'll be dead or past it so it won't be their problem."

"Look," she said in a stony voice. "Here's the fall of Babylon and its ramparts tumbling down."

"The fall of Babylon. It's still not too late, not quite,

but we've got to act *now*. How *can* you be so defeatist, Adele?"

"Oh, Brendan," she groaned. "You've got a one-track mind."

"A one-track mind," he muttered, drawing her to him, then slid his fingers down inside her shorts and grabbed a spiteful handful.

She gasped.

"We're on CCTV," she hissed, wriggling out of his grip.

"You look like an angry bush baby," he hissed back.

She stalked on a few meters ahead, and even her pale legs looked indignant in the gloom.

"Sorry," he whispered when he had caught up with her. He did not feel sorry; he felt angry and cruel.

"A plague of frogs," she snapped, staring ahead. "You'll like the next one, I bet. Armageddon."

Despite himself he was peering closely at the forces of hell, the scimitars and swords and charging horsemen, the blade-shaped flames in the sky.

"So that's Armageddon," he said. "Not exactly convincing, though, is it. A bit tame."

"You'd prefer the real thing," she said, furious. "You'd rather be cycling round the battlefields of Normandy."

"I bet they thought *that* was Armageddon at the time," he said. "But it wasn't."

"Yes, you liked that Musée des Blindés in Saumur," she added nastily. "The tank museum."

"It wasn't actually that interesting. It was quite disappointing, really. Though there was an FT-17 Renault from 1917."

She had stayed outside and watched the bikes while he'd gone round the museum in the company of what looked mainly like ex-army types and their tired wives. She had been able to hear the taped military music, brashly jaunty and tear-jerking, male voices swinging along in enthusiastic company, drum rolls and crude trumpet voluntaries.

"It happens, war," said Brendan. "It's major. It's part of life."

"I do know that, geography boy."

"Though if we get a proper global treaty on this, it could mean the end of war altogether. You'd like that, wouldn't you?"

"Huh. I don't think *that's* going to happen."

"What? The global treaty? Or the end of war?"

"Both. Neither. Look, Brendan, I'm sure you're right about it all, the climate stuff, but the thing is, the world doesn't want to cut back. In fact, the world thinks it's *wrong* to cut back. Can't you see that? What the world wants is economic growth. Increased productivity. The world won't listen to a word you say. You know that."

"Even if it means the end of the world?"

"Yup. Even if it means that."

"But—"

"Look. Last one. The New Jerusalem. Happy ending. Time to go."

"Wait, Adele," he cajoled, taking her hand. "Look. Look, it's a lovely white château! Circular towers and crenellations and lancet windows. Your favorite sort!" She stood, head averted, her hand rigid in his. "All the flowers and fruit trees are back in action—I bet they're organic—and it's floating between land and sky," he crooned.

He caught a flicker of a smile at the corner of her mouth.

"Sorry," he whispered, and this time he really did feel something, a stirring, though it wasn't exactly remorse.

She gave his fingers a faint squeeze. Hand in hand, blinking, they emerged into the late-afternoon sunlight.

For their last night they had put euros aside for a meal in a proper restaurant. The rest of the holiday it had been peaches and tomatoes, a baguette and some cheese, and evening picnics on park benches or under trees until the dark drove them back to whichever hostel they were staying in.

Now they sat in unaccustomed formality across the table from each other with a candle between them casting a glow. On the wall beside their table was a machine-stitched hanging of a medieval hunting scene.

"A bit feeble, isn't it, after the real thing," said Brendan as they examined its pastel stags and undifferentiated trees. "I can't believe we're going home tomorrow. Who will I talk to without you there?" He grabbed her hand and gave it a hasty kiss.

What still surprised both of them was the ease with which they had spoken to each other from the start and how they had not run out of things to talk about, even though they had been together exclusively now for ten days without a break. In fact, it felt like they had only just started. It was as if all this was only the beginning of a much longer conversation between them.

"I'm going to have to apply for another loan when I get back," said Brendan. "I really hope I can get a decent amount of work this August. September."

"Snap," said Adele. "Eighteen thousand. More than, probably, by the end of finals."

"Worth it, though, if you get a decent degree. Of course, we're rich compared to most of the world."

"I do know that," she said. You're not my conscience, she did not need to add. There had been several dangerous semisubmerged rocks, she reminded herself, in the broadly halcyon sea of this holiday. His tendency to lecture made her want to turn on her heel and walk away.

"Sorry," he said, touching her hand again. "Stop me when I do that."

"Thanks," she smiled. "I will."

It delighted her, their fluidity, how open and interested in each other they were, checking and clashing and counterbalancing. By this process, they had been leading each other into unanticipated fields of fresh thought and feeling. She still thought him misguided, though, if he imagined he could change anything about the future.

"*Onglet à l'échalotes.* That's steak, isn't it?" said Brendan uncertainly, studying the menu. "*Civet de marcassin.* Wild boar casserole. I might have the steak."

"I thought meat was as bad as coal. Especially steak," said Adele, who called herself a pescatarian. "*Barbue.* What's *barbue*? Oh, brill. What's brill?"

"There aren't exactly plenty more fish in the sea, either."

"We could have the vegetable soup."

"Yes. Cheaper, too," he said, brightening. "Then the *tian de courgettes,* whatever a *tian* is."

"And they've got profiteroles. My favorite. I'm going to have profiteroles if I have room. Funny, that monster in the tapestry this afternoon made me think of profiteroles."

"What monster?"

"The Beast of the Sea." She thought back to the weird tapestry creature and its long thick stalky neck supporting the pyramid cluster of multiple lions' heads. Each of these seven round faces had worn a nasty smile of its own.

"Like a croquembouche," she added.

"A croquembouche?"

"My aunt had one when she got married, instead of a wedding cake. It's a pyramid of profiteroles stuck together with caramel."

We could have a croquembouche when we get married, Brendan caught himself thinking and turned red. It wasn't that he wanted her to agree with him all the time; in fact, he positively relished most of the differences between them. But when, that afternoon, it had come to the one thing he was most passionate about and she had refused to listen, he hadn't been able to help himself from falling into a pit of anger.

"I've got something of a monster in me," he said now. "I can't believe I was like that with you at the end there, in the gallery. The beer at lunch didn't help, but that's no excuse. Anger. That's my monster."

Just then their food arrived, and for some minutes there was no more talk, only chewing and swallowing and appreciative little noises.

"My monster is melancholy," she admitted after a while.

"That's not a monster."

"Yes it is. It really is. I've got to fight it."

"I'll help you."

"All right. For example. I can't see any future."

"We could live in a cave." He grinned. "Like those troglodytes in Chinon."

"Nobody our age will ever be able to afford a cave, even."

"A tent, then. We're bound to be allowed to pitch our tent in some old person's backyard. We don't need much, we could grow stuff, grow our own food—"

"Not lemons," she said. "Or bananas."

"No, not them, obviously. But we could grow all the stuff the monks were growing in that garden at Villandry, remember? All those cabbages and lettuces and zucchinis. We could make *tians* every night! You're so beautiful. When I look at you, I know I could do anything."

"That's why I haven't been wanting to listen to your plans, Brendan. The trouble is, I don't think they're going to work. I wish I'd chosen Human Rights for my special topic; all that reading I did for The End of the World was just too much."

"I know, I know," he said. "But think! Those guys who stitched that tapestry back there, it must have looked the same to them; they must have thought the world hadn't got long, what with the Black Death, and famine, and the clergy threatening them with plagues of monsters. And that was seven hundred years ago."

"True."

"Also, I feel happier than I ever have in my life."

"Do you?" she said and smiled a watery smile. "Why?"

"I'm with you." He shrugged.

. . .

Outside was warm and darkly velvet. They started the walk back to the hostel at a languorous pace, under a star-packed sky. He stopped to kiss her, and their tongues tasted of the wine they had drunk at dinner, the light strawberry-red Chinon.

"I wish this wasn't the last night," she murmured into his shoulder. She felt a lurch of concern at the thought of him alone, his sudden scowls misunderstood by others, his sanguine sunny breadth ignored or wasted.

"But we're not over just because the holiday is," he said.

"I thought last night when we were, um, you know, that I didn't want that ever to be over. But I knew it would be. Same with the meal just now; while I was enjoying it I knew that would be over in a little while too."

"And one day we're all going to die!" he said. "But not yet. Just because we're going to die one day doesn't spoil being alive, does it?"

"Everything's always got to be over in the end."

"You're like Pandora. You need to look on the bright side. Think outside the box, Pandora!"

"That's great, coming from you. You're the one who's going round setting end dates." She pulled away. "Sorry. Not that again. Look, there's the Big Dipper, and there's Orion with three stars in his belt."

I'm not a gloom-and-doom merchant, Adele, he wanted to say. You know I'm not; in fact, I'm a sight more of an optimist than you are.

He doesn't need to convince me, she thought. I know what he's saying. I just think it's hopeless and we're the last generation. The last but one, to be more accurate. Our children will be the last. That's my considered opinion as an historian, is it? Yes, it is.

"What I think," he said carefully, "what I think is, if you really want something to happen, to change, then that definitely improves the chances of it actually coming true."

"Sounds reasonable. I can see the sense in that. Yes."

"Good. So . . ."

"I can't promise anything," she responded, with equal care. "Or, rather, I can. I promise I won't close my ears again. That was stupid of me this afternoon. I'm sorry."

"That's good enough for me," he murmured. He wrapped his arms round her again and poked the tip of his tongue into first one of her ears and then the other. She closed her eyes and sighed.

"Listen," he whispered, his breath rustling in her hair. "I know what I want, Adele."

Something had shifted in his voice, in the temperature of the microclimate that enveloped them, and it roused her to pull away and hold him at arm's length.

"No," she said. "Don't say it."

She put her hand up to his mouth to stop the words from coming out.

"Why not?" he spluttered, after a struggle.

"It's too soon," she said. "It might not be true."

"Can I say it in French?"

"No."

"Then I'll think it instead," he said, holding her hard. "I'll dream it at night and I'll think it in the day."

She was twisting and turning, trying to struggle out of his arms. He enjoyed these tussles more than she did, she realized; he liked a challenge. She looked up, frowning, into his delighted face.

"Why are you smiling?"

"I can smile, can't I? There isn't any law against smiling, is there?"

He ran several steps ahead of her and skipped round, playing air guitar.

"I'm a troubadour!" he sang. "I'm a troubadour!"

She ran after him, caught between laughter and protest.

"Look at the stars!" he yelled. "Hello, Wormwood! Come in, Wormwood, are you receiving me? OK, the universe is huge, we don't matter, all that. . . . So what?"

"It's no use," she panted, lunging at him and missing.

"So what," he shouted, running ahead of her. "So

what so what so what! You can't stop me from saying it! I'm going to say it!"

"Don't!" she called, running after him. "Don't say it! Kiss me, though."

"I'll do that," he said, lifting her into the air and letting her slide slowly down the front of his body. "I'll do more than that."

He lifted her again and whirled her in his arms until they were both dizzy. Breathing hard, exhilarated, they leaned into a mutual embrace, this time for balance as much as anything. Then they stood in the fathomless dark and stared saucer-eyed beyond the stratosphere into the night, as troupes of boisterous planets wheeled across the blackness all round them.

Channel 17

I

"That was definitely her in the Eurostar line," says Paul from the small double where he lies zapping the television atop the wardrobe with a remote control.

"It certainly looked like her," says Jackie, rezipping their suitcase and stowing it behind the door. "Despite the sunglasses. Oh if the children think they can hold wild parties while the cat's away, I'll kill them."

"Being very friendly with that bloke who definitely wasn't her husband," says Paul. "Seventeen channels but they're all in French."

"Imagine if they were staying at this hotel," says Jackie. "Imagine if we bumped into them at breakfast."

"A nasty shock," Paul agrees. "That's what Paris is

for, though, isn't it? That's what it *means* to the English. Somewhere where you won't get caught."

"Oh the French think we're ridiculous," says Jackie. "Apparently they take all that in stride over here. They even have a sort of happy hour when it's allowed, late in the afternoon—they call it the peccadillo or something."

"Isn't that Spanish, *peccadillo*?" queries Paul. "*Jalapeño? Siesta?* Anyway, it's probably all just talk. Hot air."

"And instead of screaming and crying and divorce they do that French shrug and say *tant pis,*" continues Jackie, joining him on the bed. "Have you got to Channel 17 yet? It says it's the adult channel, on this card."

"Give me that," he says. "Oh. It's nonpaying. It won't be any good if it's free."

"So," she says, fitting herself into his side. "You know about these things, do you."

On the screen on top of the wardrobe a girl in meager underwear is slowly drawing a thin white stocking up her leg. When it covers her thigh at last, she starts to roll it off again, very gradually, with stoic deliberation.

"Is that *it*?" he says as they watch the girl repeat the process, easing on the white stocking, a centimeter at a time, along her outstretched leg. "And why's she wearing sunglasses?"

"She's probably Albanian, poor girl," says Jackie.

"She doesn't want her mother to recognize her. Turn it off."

"But it's so *boring*," he complains, mesmerized.

"Turn it *off* then," she says, seizing the remote. "Our first night away alone together in five years and you're still watching television. Come here."

"No, hold on, Jackie, I'm bushed. No, no, really I am. Oof. Let's have a rest first."

After a pause Jackie says, "It used to be the men who had the affairs, ten years ago, when the children were little. But now that we're older, it's the women."

"I've never had an affair," says Paul.

"No," says Jackie. "I'd know if you had. I'm more than enough for you. I'm as much as you can manage."

"You're my best friend," says Paul, with a mighty yawn and a smile.

"Snap," says Jackie. "But do you think that might be because we both work full-time and, what with office life and the children, we've got nothing left for anybody else?"

"I don't know," says Paul. "I don't care. All I know is, it works."

"Because friendships need to be kept in repair like anything else. Like the house. Paul, d'you think we can leave the windows another year? Or are they at the point of no return? Paul?"

A gentle snore alerts her to the fact that he has fallen asleep with his arms round her. She lies like this for a while until the light starts to fade, then gently detaches herself and creeps off to the bathroom for a shower. I say something, he says something back, she thinks as she stands under the stream of hot water. Sometimes that modifies my view and sometimes his; or we agree to disagree. She closes her eyes and lets the water pour onto her face. It's like a long-running conversation, she thinks. It's gone on for decades and it doesn't look like it's about to stop now.

She wraps herself in a towel and goes to lie down beside him on the bed again.

"Hello," he says, opening his eyes and smiling. "You look different outside the house."

"Do I?"

"Yes."

"No fancy underwear I'm afraid," she says as he unwraps her.

"That's all right."

"Oh come here," she says.

II

In the next room along, a woman lounges on the small double divan, slightly slippery under her kimono from the rose-and-black-pepper hydrating oil she added to her bath an hour ago. She is reading a restaurant-review printout from the computer in the hotel lobby, looking up the tricky words in the French dictionary Donald sent her last week along with the Eurostar ticket. He should be here any minute now if all goes according to plan.

This one looks promising, a Michelin star in the Place Denfert-Rochereau. She loves the very sound of Paris, even the metro names: Ménilmontant; Mairie des Lilas; Bréguet-Sabin. Not that she intends to use the metro this weekend, absolutely not. The various heels she has packed to lift her toward Donald's gray eminence are hardly sidewalk wear.

"Les papilles," she says, wrinkling her brow and riffling through the dictionary. "Tastebuds. Oh. And *la vie de patachon?* A rollicking or wild life. *Patachon!* Very me." She pushes the dictionary aside and lights a cigarette, then picks up the remote and starts to channel-hop.

He's mad about her. She can make him groan just by looking at him. And it's about time in her life for her to stand up and say, No, look here, for once I'm doing something for *me.* On the television screen on top of the wardrobe a seminaked girl in Ray-Bans is easing a white stocking down her leg. How tacky, thinks the woman, how low-budget. Channel 17! She's even got cellulite unless that's a shadow. She stretches her own bare polished leg in the air and gloats. "I just want to be adored," she whispers. Donald's wife gave up years ago, she refuses point-blank. She only cares about the children now, it's all sublimated. Which is fine for her, but not exactly very fair on Donald, who is an extremely physical man as well as highly successful.

Aiming the remote again, she makes the girl disappear, white stockings and all. But stockings wouldn't be a bad idea, she thinks, and roots through her suitcase until she finds a pair. She also extracts the lime-green balconnet number with detachable turquoise straps and tries this on too, posing in front of the mirror, peering back over her shoulder at her rear view and narrowing her eyes with satisfaction.

What she finds hard to take is the censorious line people assume when they know nothing about the facts at all. Marriage may be a contract, but it's not the same as buying a house, she thinks, growing hot with indignation at the memory of that talk with her so-called friend Clare. Just because you marry someone when you're twenty-three it doesn't mean you've bagged them for good. It's not like getting up early and putting your towel on a sunbed, for goodness' sake!

When her own marriage had stopped working she had refused to compromise. They were no longer in love, it was going nowhere, it was time to split. Her mother had had the nerve to tell her to "stick at it," as though the smugness of a tight little nuclear family was worth selling your soul for. Alfie, who had been two at the time, had barely noticed what was happening. It was absolutely typical of her mother when last year at the age of seventy-three she had announced that she was leaving Daddy—"Better late than never" was her excuse. Unbelievably selfish, with his second hip operation in the offing. Alfie was staying with her this weekend as it happened. Anyway, most of the children in his class were on the move on weekends between stepmothers and half sisters and demi-grandparents. It was the new version of the extended family, and who was to say it was any worse than the old claustrophobic sort? So get over it.

Donald had been great with Alfie, the time he'd met him. He adored his own three daughters, made no secret of the fact, to the point of tears in his eyes. Maybe we'll have a baby, she'd said to sooth him the last time he'd gotten upset; a little boy, a baby brother for your girls. And it wasn't all one-sided. *She'd* have to give things up too: her beautiful flat, her transformation pad as she called it; having her own space.

Sitting cross-legged on the bed she zaps the shooter at the television again, then slews herself slowly into a spinal twist; holding it, she watches the girl on the screen point her toes and reinsert them into the rolled-up white stocking. Sure, it'll be messy. But she is prepared for that. She will see him through it, support him in every way she can. That might just be the price of passion, mightn't it?

The telephone rings. There is a gentleman in reception to see her.

"I'm expecting him," she smiles, turning off the television, checking herself in the mirror. "Tell him to come up."

III

A moment after this the third door along the corridor bursts open and a magnificently scowling young man strides off toward the lift. Peeping round the door frame appears a woman with a baby. "Where are you going?" she calls after him. "Out," comes the reply.

"He wants it to be like it was before," she murmurs to the baby, retreating back into the room. "He wants it to be as if nothing has happened. He wants me to agree to a babysitter I haven't met, organized by the hotel, for tonight, and I won't. 'This was supposed to be a romantic weekend,' he says, 'but you're in love with *him* not me.' "

"And the thing is," she croons, lifting the baby and planting kisses in his delighted neck, "he's right."

It hurts like a punch in the stomach that he has been so dramatic, so violent, walking out on them like that, and tears stand in her eyes; but at the same time she is almost too tired to care.

"I've lost you," he'd shouted, just before storming off. "You're lost to me."

"No you haven't," she'd bleated. "No I'm not," wanting to add, Don't be such a baby.

She knows where he has gone. He's gone to find Samuel Beckett's grave in the Cimitierè du Montparnasse. She knows this because earlier that afternoon they went for a walk in the Jardin du Luxembourg instead. They pushed the pram along the gravel paths of palm trees and pony rides, past the octagonal boating lake and the old men playing *boules;* and he had looked round restlessly and quoted from "First Love."

"Can't you enjoy it here, now?" she'd asked. What she didn't say was "I feel betrayed too."

" 'Personally I have no bone to pick with graveyards,' " he'd intoned. "Listen, it was one of the places I promised myself I'd visit once I finished my thesis." He had wanted a literary pilgrimage rather than a walk in the park, and now she was paying for having insisted on the latter.

She places the baby in the middle of the bed and barricades him with pillows. He waves his bare legs in the air, then begins to fuss and grumble. He wants to be fed. Has she got time to unpack her sponge bag, wash her face even, before he starts to cry in earnest? Probably not. She rearranges the pillows into a mound for her back and leans against them while he commences huffing and puffing to get at her. In the wall

mirror above the desk she catches sight of her reflection, chalk pale with dark half-moons beneath her
eyes, his soft head bobbing away at a bosom hard and
veined as marble.

"Ah," she groans as he latches on. The broad-chested
little boy gasps and gulps in his eagerness for the milk,
and she murmurs, "Slowly, sweetheart, slowly."

After a while he goes at her less greedily. In a few
minutes he will fall asleep, sated, and to make sure
she doesn't fall asleep before he does she flicks on the
television with the remote control. Pressing the Mute
button, she surfs through noiseless images of washing
machines, war zones, ice cream gâteaux and open-heart
surgery until she reaches Channel 17 at last, where
there is an altogether less agitating scene of someone
getting undressed. How lovely, she thinks, watching
the solitary girl take her time; how wonderful to have
the bed to yourself.

Much later the young man unlocks the door and finds
his wife and baby sleeping deeply in the dark. He sees
them in the starry light cast by the wardrobe-perched
television set, curled round each other, oblivious to his
change of mood. Up on the screen a girl is drawing a
thin white stocking up her leg. He stands and gapes
at her. The stocking covers her thigh at last and the
girl pauses and dips her head; then she starts to ease it
down all over again, very slowly, with infinite patience.

Homework

I can't do it," groaned George, bringing his forehead to rest on the block of lined paper in front of him.

"Can't do what?" I asked, looking up from peeling the carrots for the evening meal. I work from home, so I'm round when George gets in from school. He sits at the kitchen table and I bring some milk in his Manchester United mug and a plate with a teatime snack. This might be a slice of toast and honey with a peeled satsuma from which I have removed any stray threads of pith, or perhaps an apple, cored and cut into fine slices, with a few cubes of cheddar.

Quite often I'm not able to stop what I'm doing, and then I have to stay put. I call out from my desk to say hello when I hear the front door. He calls hello back and makes his way to the television. I'd rather catch up on work in the evening but there's not always a choice.

"Can't do what?" I repeated. "I'm sure you can."

"You don't *know*. Everybody says it's really hard. And now I've got to hand it in for tomorrow."

"Why do you do this? Why do you leave it to the last minute?"

That's another wonderful thing about George—you can tell him off and he won't immediately go into orbit like some I could mention. He's not a great one for flying off the handle.

"It's just so hard," he moaned.

"Now come on," I said, drying my hands and patting his nice strong shoulder. "Sit up and tell me what it is. You never know, I might be able to help."

"It's Mr. Mottram," he said, heaving himself up from his slump. "It's English so it should be all right but he still wants to make it hard. We've got to do three sides of A4 out of our own heads."

He is already taller than me and can lift me off the ground. One or two of his friends have had their growth spurt, so that I find myself deferring to the sudden height and booming voice of a boy whom last year I knew as a clear-skinned little pipsqueak.

"What is it, this terrible task he's set you?"

" 'Write About an Event That Changed Your Life,' " said George with mournful sarcasm. "*That's* what it is."

"Three pages is a lot." Then a thought occurred

to me. "You've had all the Easter holidays to do this, haven't you? And you just didn't let on about it. Now it's your first week back and the chickens have come home to roost."

"I know," he said, spreading his hands palms upward in front of him. "There's no excuse."

"What have your friends done?"

"Dylan's written about when he went to a soccer match with his uncle, Crystal Palace v Queens Park Rangers, and realized Crystal Palace was the team he wanted to follow for the rest of his life."

"I can't see how he filled three sides of A4 with that."

"He said it only took up one page even in big writing," said George. "Now he's got to, you know, pad it out. He's going to describe all the Crystal Palace matches he's been to since then, one at a time."

Serves Mr. Mottram right, I thought; I don't know what he can be expecting from a class of thirteen-year-olds. They can't know what a life-changing event is at their age. How can they know if what happened to them last year will have changed them in twenty years' time? They won't know till they get there.

"I shouldn't really help you," I said. "I should leave you to get on with it. But if I do . . ."

"Yes?" said George, propped up on his elbows, eyeing me with wary optimism.

"*If* I help you, you've got to understand it's only this once."

"Course," he said with a beaming smile of relief. "You know I'm not like that, Mum."

"Yes." I smiled back. "I do know. I trust you."

" 'Cuz you can." He shrugged.

"All right then, let's think."

I sat down at the kitchen table and watched him assume a thoughtful expression. He furrowed his brow and chewed at the end of his Biro, then caught my eye and started to giggle.

"I'd rather write about anything else in the world," he complained.

"Just think," I said. "In fifty years' time you might really want to write about the Event That Changed Your Life. In your old age you might find you're desperate to set down your memories. Look at Grandma."

My mother had recently filled half a red notebook with startlingly deadpan revelations. Her father had at the age of fourteen rejected a future as a farm laborer and walked down from Wakefield to London to find work, where at first he slept wrapped in old newspapers on benches along the Embankment. That was before he went to fight in France. *His* father had been among other things a prizefighter at country fairs, more or less on the wrong side of the law all his life.

"No," said George, shaking his head firmly. *"Boring."*

"You might find it interesting when you get older," I persisted. "I never knew that her mother, your great-grandmother, was found as a newborn baby wrapped in a flour sack on the church steps early one Sunday morning. That accounts for a lot."

I'm glad I wasn't born at a time when you had to stay with the father of your children even if he broke your jaw.

"Where was *I* born?" asked George, who knew perfectly well.

"Willesden General," I said. "Then I kept you beside me in a basket all the time for months and months. You were a lovely mild baby, like a dewdrop."

George smiled a gratified smile. "But I did cry sometimes," he prompted.

"Yes, but when you cried it just made me laugh," I said. "You didn't wail in a high-pitched way; no, it was more like the roar of a lion and then only when you wanted milk. When you were hungry, you just roared!"

He smirked at this and gave an illustrative growl.

Following his birth I'd had an urge to find out more about my family tree. After a while I gave up. It had branches and twigs and leaves in every corner of the British Isles. There were shipwrights and ropemakers in Northumberland, laborers in Lincolnshire, watchmen and peddlers and blacksmiths from Ipswich and Barnstaple and Carlisle. The further back I went, the further afield they spread out. It seemed pointless. George was from all over the place.

"Life-changing events," I said, returning to the business at hand. "Let's think of some examples."

"If you win the lottery," suggested George.

"Or lose all your money," I said. "Go bankrupt like Dad's dad. Skip the country like my uncle Colin."

"Yes," said George, pen poised, looking less hopeful.

"What would change the life of a thirteen-year-old, though, that's the question," I reminded myself. "The death of a parent, certainly, but I don't want you writing about that because it might bring bad luck."

"Jacob's mother died," commented George. "He doesn't want to talk about it."

"No," I said. "Poor Jacob. What did she die of?"

"He says cancer. But Ranjit told me it wasn't that, it was a bottle of tablets." George shrugged. "I don't know."

"No," I said again. Jacob would get by till middle age, probably, when he would step onto this death as onto the tines of a garden fork, and the solid shaft of the handle would rear up and hit him in the face.

"So, not death," I said. "Because that's the obvious one. No, it'll have to be your parents' divorce."

"But you're not divorced."

"Well, we are in this story."

"He'll think it's really true," said George, looking worried.

"So?" I said. "It'll fill three sides of A4. Let's have

the mum leaving the dad for a change, rather than the other way round. And you have to move from your family house to a flat, and your new bedroom is tiny, and you have to share with your little brother who drives you mad."

"I haven't got a little brother."

"Mr. Mottram doesn't know that."

My siblings are scattered far and wide. Sharon runs a bed-and-breakfast up by Hadrian's Wall. Valerie has an alpha-male job in the City, just like her husband, and lives in a big house in Wimbledon. Keith has had various irons in the fire over the years, but now he's teaching English as a foreign language in China. Very modern Britain, our family.

George looked at me warily. I could see he was torn between natural fantasy-hating honesty and a desire to have someone else do his homework.

"Is it allowed?" he asked.

"Yes," I said. "It's English, isn't it? Don't they call this bit creative writing? Well, you're just being creative."

"Ha," said George.

"Inventive," I added. "It's a *good* thing. Listen, you want to watch the match tonight, don't you? Chelsea v Liverpool, isn't it?"

"Yes."

"In which case you'd better get this homework finished before dinner. Which I'm doing specially for seven o'clock because I know you like all that warm-up chat beforehand."

"Thanks, Mum."

I couldn't resist giving him a hug, the roaring dewdrop baby who had grown into this broad-shouldered boy. Last week I'd been making flapjacks while he stood by to lick the spoon, and I mentioned that I'd always liked the picture of the lion on the Golden Syrup tin. " 'Out of the strong came forth sweetness,' " he read aloud, peering at the green-and-gold picture. "That's what's written underneath it." I never knew that before.

"Have you got your pen ready? I'm not going to write this for you, you know, I'm only going to give you ideas."

"OK," he agreed. He was in no position to object.

"Your parents had arguments for years. You remember the slammed doors and bitter words from when you were little," I began.

George started to write.

"You tried to blot it out but you couldn't help feeling upset inside. It got into your dreams. You could put a bad dream in, George; that would take up a few lines."

"What about?"

"Oh, an earthquake perhaps," I said. "I was always dreaming about earthquakes and floods and fires when I was your age. Or you're in a house and it falls down round you and you run but the ground opens up in front of you."

"To pad it out a bit?" said George.

"If you like. Then there's the divorce, which is a relief after all the fighting."

"Why did Auntie Sharon get divorced?"

"I don't know," I said, tutting. "They seemed quite happy to start with, but then Mike turned into a bear with a sore head when she had the twins. Some people find domestic life more of a trial than others."

"Dad loves domestic," commented George. "On Fridays when he gets back home he says, 'Ah, domestic bliss.' "

"Yes, well," I said with a stunted smile.

"Auntie Sharon lives in the nicest place and she's got three dogs but Auntie Valerie's got the best job," said George. "Her family goes on the best holidays and they've got an Audi and a BMW. I want a BMW when I get a job. That's the first thing I'll buy."

"Oh really," I sniffed. "The only time they all manage to get together as a family is when they go on some expensive safari thousands of miles away."

"Just because they've got good jobs," said George, "you shouldn't be jealous."

"I'm not jealous!" I declared. "How could I be jealous of anyone working those ridiculous hours? They've sold their souls."

"Oh Mum," said George reprovingly.

"Anyway, after the divorce, you have to move out of your house and change schools."

"Why?"

"Because you do. Money. Jobs. And you go and live with your father and your little brother, and visit your mother on weekends. You might even ask if you can go and live with your grandma for a while."

"Why?" said George again, large-eyed, even more down in the mouth.

"For a break," I said absently.

Grow up in certain homes and it's like being out on a cold choppy sea in an open dinghy with two angry fishermen in charge. Or sometimes just a single fisherman, who is, what's more, drunk. Whereas with a grandparent, life for a child can be less dangerous, more like being afloat on a reservoir.

"What happens next?"

"The mum wants a new start. She wants to see the world! Everybody else has."

"But Mum, Mr. Mottram will think it's really you."

"When you think about it," I mused, "it's none of Mr. Mottram's business. He should only be interested in it as a piece of writing. Is it a good piece of writing? Is it convincing?"

"What if he asks me," muttered George.

"He won't. He's an English teacher, isn't he, not a psychotherapist. So if he did ask you, he'd just be being nosy."

George shrugged helplessly.

When I went to live with my grandmother for a while, she had enough to eat but not enough to keep warm. She was over seventy but she had kept on at one of her old cleaning jobs, for Mrs. Nibthwaite, mainly for the sake of being in a house with central heating. I went along to help with the floors; then, while she polished and dusted, I puzzled over the Latin homework that held my enfranchisement. She never considered this work demeaning and, in fact, looked down on Mrs. Nibthwaite as an unfeminine woman, a cold woman who made her husband lonely and who did not grieve when he died but said, "Now I'm free to do what I want to do" and went off round the world on various package holidays. The cheerful bearded sailor on her packet of Player's was as close as *she* ever got to the sea. She cooked with a cigarette in her mouth; quite often ash would fall into the gravy, and she would stir it in as extra seasoning.

"Listen, you're doing *A Midsummer Night's Dream,* aren't you," I continued. "Do you think Shakespeare got asked whether he'd ever grown donkey's ears?"

George smiled briefly.

"Right. So you see your mum on weekends and one weekend she tells you she wants to go to Peru and asks if she can borrow your Duke of Edinburgh rucksack. She promises she'll send you postcards; it's just something she's got to do to move forward in her life."

George scribbled away, not happy with where the story line was going but incapable of coming up with an alternative. I felt powerful, like a magician pulling rabbits out of a hat.

"I still don't think it's allowed," he said.

"Of course it's allowed," I said. "You've got to have things happening, see, or it's not a story. Think of the films you like. Car chases. Explosions. Sharks."

"Can the mum be swimming in the China Sea and then a shark comes up?" asked George hopefully, trying to enter into the creative spirit.

"Probably not," I said drily. "That might be a step too far for Mr. Mottram, don't you think?"

"But you said—"

"Yes, but we've got to make it believable. It's like a game, isn't it. He shouldn't be able to tell what's real and what's made up."

"I'd like to go to Japan," said George. "They've got the new Nintendo Wii there and I could get it way ahead of everybody else. Plus you don't have to have injections to go there."

"Next," I said, "I think the dad meets someone else, don't you? At first he's just been going to his job and coming back and cooking nasty dinners. You've had to help—buying a loaf of bread on the way home from school, that sort of thing, and doing the washing up without being asked."

"Isn't there a dishwasher in the new place?"

"It's broken. And nobody gets round to finding someone to mend it and anyway you're all out all day. Maybe your little brother can be in because he's ill, though. Chicken pox."

"My little brother can't be left on his own," objected George. "If he's seven or eight or something. That's against the law."

"OK, you've got an older sister instead."

"*She* can cook," he said, with satisfaction. The meals were worrying him.

"No she can't," I said. "She just eats potato chips and bananas. No, it's the dad that has to do it after work, unless you start teaching yourself from a cookbook."

George looked up from his pad suspiciously. I was always trying to get him interested in cutting up broccoli florets or making omelettes.

"The dad should do it," he protested. "I'm a kid. It's not my job. Kids should be looked after by their parents."

"You're thirteen, George!" I said. I was about to bring up the walk from Wakefield, but then I stopped myself. "Oh well, it's your story. The dad does the cooking, but it's always pasta."

"Cool." George grinned.

"And the pasta is always soggy." I scowled. "Feel free to carry on."

"No, no," he said. "After you."

"He's been trying to cook, but he's no good at it.

Then he meets, let's see, Miranda. You know she's not nasty or anything but she's got nothing to do with you. And he starts including her in everything."

"How?"

"She's always there when he's round, watching television with you, in between you on the sofa."

"What, even when football's on?"

"Yes. She pretends to like it. She says she's a Chelsea supporter."

"Chelsea," said George grimly.

"One weekend your mum tells you she's off backpacking in three days' time, first stop Thailand," I continued. "We need to wind this up, George. She promises she'll send postcards. You could have them arriving a bit later on with little messages—you know, 'ate fried tortoise,' 'went bungee jumping,' that sort of thing. You could stick them on the fridge so Miranda could see them."

"Maybe *she* can cook."

"Not likely," I said. "She's not interested in food. She doesn't see why she should anyway. Why *should* she? Then it's the last straw. You've just had another of these postcards, the mum's got as far as Australia. And your dad announces that your holiday this year is camping in Wales; there's no money for anything else. He can stretch to walking boots for you and your sister but that's it."

"Wales," said George with leaden emphasis.

"I think you can leave it somewhere there," I said airily. "It's April now, just the sort of time people are planning their summer holidays. Mr. Mottram will buy that."

"But how do I finish it off?"

"You don't have to really; you don't have to solve everything. It's not a police procedural. But you're right, you do need something."

"Yes."

"I know," I said. "Pull in your love of football. All these months since the divorce you've turned to football to forget. This year you've been following the Champions League with a passion. Is your team doing all right in it? Manchester United?"

"Last night's game was *amazing,* Mum," said George earnestly. "Rooney scored this goal in the ninety-first minute and I couldn't believe it." He shook his head in wonder. "It was unbelievable."

"Was he happy?"

"He did this full-body dive all the way along the grass, then he lay with his head on his arms and they all bundled in on top of him. We were playing at home, though, so it might not be so good in the return match."

"You can put all that in, just like you've told it to me." I'd been struck by a thought. "Now, what does the Man U crowd chant when it wants them to win? You know, like Tottenham is 'Come on, you Spu-urs.' "

"UNITED! UNITED!" he chanted automatically.

"There you are," I said. "That's your last paragraph. You explain how football has got you through your parents' divorce. You describe Rooney's great goal in the ninety-first minute. How your team means so much to you. Then you write how you joined in with the TV crowd shouting, "UNITED! UNITED!" And you round it off with the words 'Ironic, really.' "

"Ha," said George, who wasn't slow on the uptake even if the pilot light of his imagination had yet to flare into action. He smiled reluctantly and started to write this down.

I looked at his fair head bent over the pad of A4. The time for advice was almost gone. Beware heat without warmth. When a man loses his temper, people say, That's the Irish in him, or the Scottish, or the Viking. Don't listen to them. "Dirty players" or "terriers" are what they call footballers with that anger-stoked edge, but strength without sweetness is no use at all.

"Ironic because . . . ?" I asked.

"The mum and the dad. They're *not* united."

"There you are."

I glanced at the kitchen clock.

"I've got to get on," I said. "I've got my own work to do."

"That's all right," he said, smiling up at me. "You go. I can do it now."

The Festival of the Immortals

The Daniel Defoe event had just been canceled, and as a consequence of this the line for the tea tent stretched halfway round the meadow. Toward the back, shivering slightly this damp October morning, were two women who looked to be somewhere in the early November of their lives.

"Excuse me, but are you going to the next talk?" one of them asked the other, waving a festival brochure at a late lost wasp.

"Who, me?" replied the woman. "Yes. Yes, I am. It's Charlotte Brontë reading from *Villette,* I believe."

"Hmm, I hope they keep the actual reading element to a minimum," said the first, wrinkling her nose. "Don't you? I can read *Villette* anytime."

"Good to hear it in her own voice, though," suggested the other.

"Oh I don't know," said the first. "I think that can be overdone. Some curiosity value, of course, but half the time an actor would read it better. No, I want to know what she's *like*. That difficult father. Terribly shortsighted. Extremely short, full stop. The life must shed light on the work, don't you think. What's the matter, have I got a smudge on my face or something?"

"It's not . . . ?" said the other, gazing at her wide-eyed. "It's not Viv Armstrong is it?"

"Yes," said Viv Armstrong, for that was indeed her name. "But I'm afraid I don't . . ."

"Phyllis!" said the other, beaming. "Phyllis Goodwin. The ATS, remember? Bryanston Square? Staining our legs brown with cold tea and drawing on the seams with an eyebrow pencil?"

"Fuzzy!" exclaimed Viv at last. "Fuzzy Goodwin!"

"Nobody's called me that for over fifty years," said Phyllis. "It was when you wrinkled your nose in that particular way, that's when I knew it was you."

The rest of their time waiting in line flew by. Before they knew it they were carrying tea and carrot cake over to a table beneath the rustling amber branches of an ancient beech tree.

"I'm seventy-eight and I'm still walking up volcanoes," Viv continued, as they settled themselves. "I don't get to the top anymore but I still go up them. I'm off to Guatemala next week."

Eager, impulsive, slapdash, Phyllis remembered. Rule-breaking. Artless. Full of energy. In some ways, of course, she must have changed, but just now, she appeared exactly, comically, as she always had been, in her essence if not in her flesh. Although even here, physically, her smile was the same, the set of her shoulders, the sharpness of nose and eyes.

"The first time I saw you, we were in the canteen," said Phyllis. "You were reading *The Waves* and I thought, Ah, a kindred spirit. I was carrying a steamed treacle pudding and I sat down beside you."

That's right, thought Viv, Fuzzy had had a sweet tooth—look at the size she was now. She'd had long yellow hair, too, just like Veronica Lake, but now it was short and white.

"I still do dip into *The Waves* every so often," she said aloud. "It's as good as having a house by the sea, don't you think? Especially as you get older. Oh, I wonder if she's on later, Virginia; I'd love to go to one of her readings."

Viv knew many writers intimately, thanks to modern biographers, but she was only really on first-name terms with members of the Bloomsbury group.

"Unfortunately not," said Phyllis. "That's a cast-iron rule of this festival, a writer can only appear if they're out of copyright, and Virginia isn't out of it for another five years."

"But she must be, surely," said Viv. "Isn't copyright fifty years?"

"Well it was, until recently," said Phyllis. "And Virginia *was* out of it by the early nineties; I happen to know because I was at one of her readings here. Oh, she was wonderful. What a talker! She kept the whole pavilion in stitches—spellbound—rocking with laughter. But then they changed the copyright law, something to do with the E.U., and now it's life plus seventy years, and she went back in again. So she won't be allowed to return until 2011 at the earliest. Very galling, as we might not still be here by then."

"Oh I don't know," said Viv. "Aren't you being rather gloomy? Seventy-eight isn't that old."

"It is quite old, though," said Phyllis doubtfully.

"Well I suppose so. But it's not *old* old," said Viv. "It's not ninety. Come on, now, Fuzzy, we've got some catching up to do."

In the next few minutes they attempted to condense the last half century into digestible morsels for each other. Viv had put in a year at teacher training college, then found teaching posts through Gabbitas-Thring, while Phyllis had taken a secretarial course at Pitman's College in Bloomsbury, followed by a cost-accounting job at the Kodak factory near where she lived, totting up columns of figures in a large ledger at a slanting desk. At some point between the Olympics being held at Wembley and the year of the Festival of Britain, they had met their respective husbands.

"All this is such outside stuff, though," said Phyllis obscurely. She was supposed to be writing her memoirs, spurred on by a local life-writing course, but had been dismayed at her attempts so far, so matter-of-fact and chirpy and boring.

They plowed on. Viv had settled just inside the M25 London Orbital, before it was there, of course, while Phyllis lived just outside it. They'd had three children each and now had seven grandchildren between them.

"Two girls and a boy," said Viv. "One's in computers, one's a physiotherapist and one has yet to find his feet. He's forty-eight."

"Oh," said Phyllis. "Well I had the other combination, two boys and a girl. Ned's an animal-feed operator but his real love is heavy metal, much good it's done him. Peter's an accountant—no, I keep forgetting, they don't call them accountants anymore. They're financial consultants now."

"Like trash collectors. 'My old man's a dustman.' Remember that?" said Viv. "Then there was 'My old man said, "Follow the van, and don't dilly dally on the way." ' My mother used to sing that. I divorced *my* old man, by the way, sometime back in the seventies."

"I'm sorry," said Phyllis.

"Don't be silly," said Viv. "I've realized I'm a natural chopper and changer. Or rather, I start off enthusiastic and then spot the feet of clay. It's a regular pattern. I did eventually find the love of my life, when I was in my sixties, but he died. What about your daughter, though? Didn't you mention a daughter?"

"Yes," said Phyllis, blinking. "Sarah. She went into the book business. In fact, she's the one who dreamed up the idea behind this festival, and now she runs it. Artistic director of the Festival of Immortals, that's her title."

"Good Lord," said Viv. "The opportunities there are for girls these days!"

"It's a full-time, year-round job, as you can imagine," said Phyllis, gaining confidence. "She spent months this year trying to persuade Shakespeare to run a workshop but the most she could get him to do was half-promise to give a master class in the sonnet. He's supposed to be arriving by helicopter at four this afternoon, but it's always touch-and-go with him, she says, it's impossible to pin him down."

"Good Lord," said Viv again and listened enthralled, as Phyllis told her anecdotes from previous years: the time Rabbie Burns had kept an adoring female audience waiting forty minutes and had eventually been tracked down in the stationery closet deep in congress or whatever he called it with Sarah's young assistant, Sophie. Then there was the awful day Sarah had introduced a reading as being from *The Floss on the Mill* and George Eliot had looked so reproachful, even more so than usual, but Sarah did tend to reverse her words when flustered; it wasn't intentional. Every year Alexander Pope roared up in a fantastic high-powered low-slung sports car, always a new one, always the latest model. Everybody looked forward to that. Jane Austen could be very sarcastic in interviews if you asked her a question she didn't like. She'd said something very rude to Sarah last year, very cutting, when Sarah had questioned her on what effect she thought being fostered by a wet nurse had had on her. Because of course that was what people were interested in now, that sort of detail, there was no getting away from it.

Last year had been really fascinating, if a bit morbid. They'd taken illness as their theme—Fanny Burney on the mastectomy she'd undergone without anesthetic, Emily Brontë giving a riveting description of the time she was bitten by a rabid dog and how she'd gone straight back home and heated up a fire iron and used it herself to cauterize her arm. Emily had been very good in the big round-table discussion, too, the one called "TB and Me," very frank. People had got the wrong idea about her, Sarah said, she wasn't unfriendly, just rather shy; she was lovely when you got to know her.

"They've done well, our children, when you think

of it," commented Viv. "But then, there was no reason for them not to. First generation to go to university."

Phyllis had tried to describe in her memoir how angry and sad she had been at having to leave school at fourteen; how she'd just missed the 1944 Education Act, with its free secondary schooling for everyone. Books had been beyond her parents' budget, but with the advent of paperbacks as she reached her teens she had become a reader. Why couldn't she find a way to make this sound interesting?

"Penny for your thoughts, Fuzzy," said Viv.

"Viv," said Phyllis, "Would you mind not calling me that? I never did like that name, and it's one of the things I'm pleased to have left in the past."

"Oh!" said Viv. "Right you are."

"Because names do label you," said Phyllis. "I mean, Phyllis certainly dates me."

"I was called Violet until I left home," confessed Viv. "Then I changed to Viv and started a new life."

"I always assumed Viv was short for Vivien," said Phyllis. "Like Vivien Leigh. I saw *Gone with the Wind* five times. Such a shame about her and Laurence Olivier."

"Laurence Olivier as Heathcliff!" exclaimed Viv. "Mr. Darcy. Henry V. Henry V! That was my first proper Shakespeare, that film."

"Mine, too," confessed Phyllis. "Then later, I was

reading 'The Whitsun Weddings'—I'd been married myself for a while—and I came to the last verse and there it was, that shower of arrows fired by the English bowmen, just like in the film. The arrows were the new lives of the young married couples on the train and it made me cry, it made me really depressed, that poem."

"Not what you'd call a family man, Philip Larkin," said Viv.

"Not really," said Phyllis. "You know, thinking about it, the only time I stopped reading altogether was when they were babies. Three under five. I couldn't do that again."

"I *did* keep reading," said Viv. "But there were quite a few accidents. And I was always an instant mashed potatoes sort of housewife, if I'm honest."

"I wish I had been," said Phyllis enviously.

She cast her mind back to all that: the hours standing over the old-style washing machine, the hundred ways with ground meat, nagging the children to clean out the guinea pig cage, collecting her repeat prescription for Valium. That time, too, she had tried to record in her memoir, but it had been even more impossible to describe than the days of her girlhood.

"It's not in the books we've read, is it, how things have been for us," said Viv. "There's only Mrs. Ramsay, really, and she's hardly typical."

"I've been bound by domestic ties," said Phyllis, "But I'm still a feminist."

"Are you?" said Viv, impressed.

"Well I do think women should have the vote so yes, I suppose I am. Because a lot of people don't really, underneath, think women should have the vote, you know."

"I had noticed," said Viv.

"It's taken me so long to notice how the world works that I think I should be allowed extra time," said Phyllis.

At this point she decided to confide in Viv about her struggles with life writing. For instance, all she could remember about her grandmother was that she was famous for having once thrown a snowball into a fried-fish shop; but was that the sort of thing that was worth remembering? Another problem was, just as you didn't talk about yourself in the same way you talked about others, so you couldn't *write* about yourself from the outside either. Not really. Which reminded her: there had been such a fascinating event here last year; Sarah had been interviewing Thomas Hardy and it had come out that he'd written his own biography, in the third person, and got his wife, Florence, to pretend that *she'd* written it! He'd made her promise to bring it out as her own work after he died. The audience had been quite indignant, but, as he told Sarah, he didn't want to be summed up by anybody else; he didn't want to be cut and dried and skewered on a spit. How would *you* like it, he'd asked Sarah, and she'd had to agree she wouldn't. This year she, Sarah, had taken care to give him a less contentious subject altogether—he was appearing tomorrow with Coleridge and Katherine Mansfield at an event called "The Notebook Habit."

"Yes," said Viv, "I've got a ticket for that."

This whole business of misrepresentation was one of Sarah's main bugbears at the festival, Phyllis continued. She found it very difficult knowing how to handle the hecklers. Ottoline Morrell, for example, turned up at any event where D. H. Lawrence was appearing, carrying on about *Women in Love,* how she wasn't Hermione Roddice, how she'd never have thrown a paperweight at anyone, how dare he and all the rest of it. Sarah had had to hire discreet security guards because of incidents like that. The thing was, people minded about posterity. They minded about how they would be remembered.

"Not me," said Viv.

"Really?" said Phyllis.

"I'm more than what's happened to me or where I've been," said Viv. "I know that, and I don't care what other people think. I can't be read like a book. And I'm not dead yet, so I can't be summed up or sum myself up. Things might change."

"Goodness," said Phyllis, amazed.

"Call no man happy until he is dead." Viv shrugged, glancing at her watch. "And now it's time for Charlotte Brontë. I had planned to question her about those missing letters to Constantin Heger, but I don't want Sarah's security guards after me."

The two women started to get up, brushing cake crumbs from their skirts and assembling bags and brochures.

"Look, there's Sarah now," said Phyllis, pointing toward the pavilion.

Linking arms, they began to make their way across the meadow to where the next line was forming.

"And look, that must be Charlotte Brontë with her, in the bonnet." Viv gestured. "See, I was right! She *is* short."

Diary of an Interesting Year

12TH FEBRUARY 2040

My thirtieth birthday. G gave me this little spiral-backed notebook and a Biro. It's a good present, hardly any rust on the spiral and no water damage to the paper. I'm going to start a diary. I'll keep my hand-writing tiny to make the paper go further.

15TH FEBRUARY 2040

G is really getting me down. He's in his element. They should carve it on his tombstone—"I Was Right."

23RD FEBRUARY 2040

Glad we don't live in London. The Hatchwells have got cousins staying with them, they trekked up from

144   ·

Peckham (three days). Went round this afternoon and they were saying the thing that finally drove them out was the sewage system—when the drains backed up it overflowed everywhere. They said the smell was unbelievable, the streets were swimming in it, and of course the hospitals are down so there's nothing to be done about the cholera. Didn't get too close to them in case they were carrying it. They lost their two sons like that last year.

"You see," G said to me on the way home, "capitalism cared more about its children as accessories and demonstrations of earning power than for their future."

"Oh shut up," I said.

2ND MARCH 2040

Can't sleep. I'm writing this instead of staring at the ceiling. There's a mosquito in the room, I can hear it whining close to my ear. Very humid, air like filthy soup, plus we're supposed to wear our face masks in bed too but I was running with sweat so I ripped mine off just now. Got up and looked at myself in the mirror on the landing—ribs like a fence, hair in greasy rats' tails. Yesterday the rats in the kitchen were busy gnawing away at the bread bin—they didn't even look up when I came in.

6TH MARCH 2040

Another quarrel with G. OK, yes, he was right, but

why crow about it? That's what you get when you marry your professor from Uni—wall-to-wall pontificating from an older man. "I saw it coming—any fool could see it coming especially after the Big Melt," he brags. "Thresholds crossed, cascade effect, hopelessly optimistic to assume we had till 2060, blahdy blahdy blah, the plutonomy as lemming, democracy's massive own goal." No wonder we haven't got any friends.

He cheered when rationing came in. He's the one who volunteered first as car-share warden for our road: one piddling little Peugeot for the entire road. He gets a real kick out of the camaraderie round the standpipe.

—I'll swap my big tin of chickpeas for your little tin of sardines.

—No, no, my sardines are protein.

—Chickpeas are protein too, plus they fill you up more. Anyway, I thought you still had some tuna.

—No, I swapped that with Astrid Huggins for a tin of tomato soup.

Really sick of bartering, but hard to know how to earn money since the Internet went down. "Also, money's no use unless you've got shedloads of it," as I said to him in bed last night, "The top layer hanging on inside their plastic bubbles of filtered air while the rest of us shuffle round with goiters and tumors and bits of old sheet tied over our mouths. Plus, we're soaking wet the whole time. We've given up on umbrellas, we just go round permanently drenched." I only stopped ranting when I heard a snore and clocked he was asleep.

8TH APRIL 2040

Boring morning washing out rags. No wood for hot water, so had to use ashes and lye again. Hands very sore even though I put plastic bags over them. Did the face masks first, then the rags from my period. Took forever. At least I haven't got to do diapers like Lexi and Esme, that would send me right over the edge.

27TH APRIL 2040

Just back from Maia's. Seven months. She's very frightened. I don't blame her. She tried to make me promise I'd take care of the baby if anything happens to her. I havered (mostly at the thought of coming between her and that throwback Martin—she'd got a new black eye, I didn't ask). I suppose there's no harm in promising if it makes her feel better. After all it wouldn't exactly be taking on a responsibility—I give a new baby three months max in these conditions. Diarrhea, basically.

14TH MAY 2040

Can't sleep. Bites itching, trying not to scratch. Heavy thumps and squeaks just above, in the ceiling. Think of something nice. Soap and hot water. Fresh air. Condoms! Sick of being permanently on knife edge re pregnancy.

Start again. Wandering round a supermarket—warm, gorgeously lit—corridors of open fridges full of tiger prawns and filet mignon. Gliding off down the fast lane in a sports car, stopping to fill up with ten gallons of gas. Online, booking tickets for *The Mousetrap,* click, ordering a case of wine, click, a holiday home, click, a pair of patent leather boots, click, a gap year, click. I go to iTunes and download *The Marriage of Figaro,* then I chat face-to-face in real time with G's parents in Sydney. No, don't think about what happened to them. Horrible. Go to sleep.

21ST MAY 2040

Another row with G. He blew my second candle out, he said one was enough. It wasn't though, I couldn't see to read anymore. He drives me mad—it's like living with a policeman. It always was, even before the Collapse. "The earth has enough for everyone's need, but not for everyone's greed" was his favorite. Nobody likes being labeled greedy. I called him Killjoy and he didn't like that. "Every one of us takes about twenty-five thousand breaths a day," he told me. "Each breath removes oxygen from the atmosphere and replaces it with carbon dioxide." Well, pardon me for breathing! What was I supposed to do—turn into a tree?

6TH JUNE 2040

Went round to the Lumleys for the news last night. Whole road there squashed into front room, straining to listen to radio—batteries very low (no new ones in the last govt delivery). Big news though—compulsory billeting next week. The Shorthouses were up in arms, Kai shouting and red in the face, Lexi in tears. "You work all your life" etc., etc. What planet is he on. None of us too keen, but nothing to be done about it. When we got back, G checked our stash of tins under the bedroom floorboards. A big rat shot out and I screamed my head off. G held me till I stopped crying then we had sex. Woke in the night and prayed not to be pregnant, though God knows who I was praying to.

12TH JUNE 2040

Visited Maia this afternoon. She was in bed, her legs have swollen up like balloons. On at me again to promise about the baby and this time I said yes. She said Astrid Huggins was going to help her when it started—Astrid was a nurse once, apparently, not really the hands-on sort but better than nothing. Nobody else on the road will have a clue what to do now we can't Google it. "All I remember from old films is that you're supposed to boil a kettle," I said. We started to laugh, we got a bit hysterical. Knuckledragger Martin put his head round the door and growled at us to shut it.

1ST JULY 2040

First billet arrived today by army truck. We've got a Spanish group of eight including one old lady, her daughter and twin toddler grandsons (all pretty feral), plus four unsmiling men of fighting age. A bit much since we only have two bedrooms. G and I tried to show them round but they ignored us, the grandmother bagged our bedroom straight off. We're under the kitchen table tonight. I might try to sleep on top of it because of the rats. We couldn't think of anything to say—the only Spanish we could remember was *muchas gracias,* and as G said, we're certainly not saying *that.*

2ND JULY 2040

Fell off the table in my sleep. Bashed my elbow. Covered in bruises.

3RD JULY 2040

G depressed. The four Spaniards are bigger than him, and he's worried that the biggest one, Miguel, has his eye on me (with reason, I have to say).

4TH JULY 2040

G depressed. The grandmother found our tins under the floorboards and all but danced a flamenco. Miguel punched G when he tried to reclaim a tin of sardines and since then his nose won't stop bleeding.

6TH JULY 2040

Last night under the table G came up with a plan. He thinks we should head north. Now that this lot is in the flat and a new group from Tehran promised next week, we might as well cut and run. Scotland's heaving, everyone else has already had the same idea, so he thinks we should get on one of the ferries to Stavanger then aim for Russia.

"I don't know," I said. "Where would we stay?"

"I've got the pop-up tent packed in a rucksack behind the shed," he said, "plus our sleeping bags and my windup radio."

"Camping in the mud," I said.

"Look on the bright side," he said. "We have a huge mortgage and we're just going to walk away from it."

"Oh, shut up," I said.

17TH JULY 2040

Maia died yesterday. It was horrible. The baby got stuck two weeks ago, it died inside her. Astrid Huggins was useless, she didn't have a clue. Martin started waving his Swiss penknife round on the second day and yelling about a cesarean, he had to be dragged off her. He's at our place now drinking the last of our precious brandy with the Spaniards. That's it. We've got to go. Now, says G. Yes.

1ST AUGUST 2040

Somewhere in Shropshire, or possibly Cheshire. We're staying off the beaten track. Heavy rain. This notebook's pages have gone all wavy. At least the Biro doesn't run. I'm lying inside the tent now, G is out foraging. We got away in the middle of the night. G slung our two rucksacks across the bike. We took turns to wheel it, then on the fourth morning we woke up and looked outside the tent flap and it was gone even though we'd covered it with leaves the night before.

"Could be worse," said G. "We could have had our throats cut while we slept."

"Oh, shut up," I said.

3RD AUGUST 2040

Rivers and streams all toxic—fertilizers, typhoid etc. So, we're following G's DIY system. Dip cooking pot into stream or river. Add three drops of bleach. Boil up on camping stove with T-shirt stretched over cooking pot. Only moisture squeezed from the T-shirt is safe to drink; nothing else. "You're joking," I said when G first showed me how to do this. But no.

9TH AUGUST 2040

Radio news in muddy sleeping bags—skeleton govt obviously struggling, they keep playing the *Enigma Variations*. Last night they announced the end of fuel for civilian use and the compulsory disabling of all remaining civilian cars. As from now we must all stay at home, they said, and not travel without permission. There's talk of martial law. We're going cross-country as much as possible—less chance of being arrested or mugged—trying to cover ten miles a day but the weather slows us down. Torrential rain, often horizontal in gusting winds.

16TH AUGUST 2040

Rare dry afternoon. Black lace clouds over yellow sky. Brown grass, frowsty gray mold, fungal frills. Dead trees come crashing down without warning—one nearly got us today, it made us jump. G was hoping we'd find stuff growing in the fields, but all the farmland round here is surrounded by razor wire and armed guards. He says he knows how to grow vegetables from his allotment days, but so what. They take too long. We're hungry *now,* we can't wait till March for some old carrots to get ripe.

22ND AUGUST 2040

G broke a front crown cracking a beechnut, there's a black hole and he whistles when he talks. "Damsons, blackberries, young green nettles for soup," he said at the start of all this, smacking his lips. He's not so keen now. No damsons or blackberries, of course—only chickweed and ivy.

He's just caught a lame squirrel so I suppose I'll have to do something with it. No creatures left except squirrels, rats and pigeons, unless you count the insects. The news says they're full of protein, you're meant to grind them into a paste, but so far we haven't been able to face that.

24TH AUGUST 2040

We met a pig this morning. It was a bit thin for a pig, and it didn't look well. G said, "Quick! We've got to kill it."

"Why?" I said. "How?"

"With a knife," he said. "Bacon. Sausages."

I pointed out that even if we managed to stab it to death with our old kitchen knife, which looked unlikely, we wouldn't be able just to open it up and find bacon and sausages inside.

"Milk, then!" said G wildly. "It's a mammal, isn't it?"

Meanwhile the pig walked off.

25TH AUGUST 2040

Ravenous. We've both got streaming colds. Jumping with fleas, itching like crazy. Weeping sores on hands and faces—the news says, unfortunate side effects from cloud seeding. What with all this and his tooth-ache (back molar, swollen jaw) and the malaria, G is in a bad way.

27TH AUGUST 2040

Found a dead hedgehog. Tried to peel off its spines and barbecue it over the last briquette. Disgusting. Both sick as dogs. Why did I use to moan about the barter system? Foraging is MUCH MUCH worse.

29TH AUGUST 2040

Dreamed of Maia and the penknife and woke up crying. G held me in his shaky arms and talked about Russia, how it's the new land of milk and honey since the Big Melt. "Some really good farming opportunities opening up in Siberia," he said through chattering teeth. "We're like in *The Three Sisters,*" I said. " 'If only we could get to Moscow.' Do you remember that production at the National? We walked by the river afterward, we stood and listened to Big Ben chime midnight." Hugged each other and carried on like this until sleep came.

31ST AUGUST 2040

G woke up crying. I held him and hushed him and asked what was the matter. "I wish I had a gun," he said.

15TH SEPTEMBER 2040

Can't believe this notebook was still at the bottom of the rucksack. And the Biro. Murderer wasn't interested in them. He's turned everything else inside out (including me). G didn't have a gun. This one has a gun.

19TH SEPTEMBER 2040

M speaks another language. Norwegian? Dutch? Croatian? We can't talk, so he hits me instead. He smells like an abandoned fridge, his breath stinks of rot. What he does to me is horrible. I don't want to think about it, I won't think about it. There's a tent and cooking stuff on the ground, but half the time we're up a tree with the gun. There's a big plank platform and a tarpaulin roped to the branches above. At night he pulls the rope ladder up after us. It's quite high—you can see for miles. He uses it for storing stuff he brings back from his mugging expeditions. I'm surrounded by tins of baked beans.

3RD OCTOBER 2040

M can't seem to get through the day without at least two blow jobs. I'm always sick afterward (sometimes during).

8TH OCTOBER 2040

M beat me up yesterday. I'd tried to escape. I shan't do that again, he's too fast.

14TH OCTOBER 2040

If we run out of beans I think he might kill me for food. There were warnings about it on the news a while back. This one wouldn't think twice. I'm just meat on legs to him. He bit me all over last night, hard. I'm covered in bite marks. I was literally licking my wounds afterward when I remembered how nice the taste of blood is, how I miss it. Strength. Calves' liver for iron. How I haven't had a period for ages. When that thought popped out I missed a beat. Then my blood ran cold.

15TH OCTOBER 2040

Wasn't it juniper berries they used to use? As in gin? Even if it was I wouldn't know what they looked like, I only remember mint and basil. I can't be pregnant. I won't be pregnant.

17TH OCTOBER 2040

Very sick after drinking rank juice off random stewed herbs. Nothing else, though, worse luck.

20TH OCTOBER 2040

Can't sleep. Dreamed of G, I was moving against him, it started to go up a little way so I thought he wasn't really dead. Dreadful waking to find M there instead.

23RD OCTOBER 2040

Can't sleep. Very bruised and scratched after today. They used to throw themselves downstairs to get rid of it. The trouble is, the gravel pit just wasn't deep enough, plus the bramble bushes kept breaking my fall. There was some sort of body down there too, seething with white maggots. Maybe it was a goat or a pig or something, but I don't think it was. I keep thinking it might have been G.

31ST OCTOBER 2040

This baby will be the death of me. Would. Let's make that a conditional. "Would," not "will."

7TH NOVEMBER 2040

It's all over. I'm still here. Too tired to

8TH NOVEMBER 2040

Slept for hours. Stronger. I've got all the food and drink, and the gun. There's still some shouting from down there but it's weaker now. I think he's almost finished.

9TH NOVEMBER 2040

Slept for hours. Fever gone. Baked beans for breakfast. More groans started up just now. Never mind. I can wait.

10TH NOVEMBER 2040

It's over. I got into his bottle of vodka, it was the demon drink that saved me. He was out mugging—left me up the tree as usual—I drank just enough to raise my courage. Nothing else worked so I thought I'd get him to beat me up. When he came back and saw me waving the bottle he was beside himself. I pretended to be drunker than I was and I lay down on the wooden platform with my arms round my head while he got the boot in. It worked. Not right away, but that night.

Meanwhile M decided he fancied a drink himself, and very soon he'd polished off the rest of it—over three-quarters of a bottle. He was singing and sobbing and carrying on, out of his tree with alcohol, and then, when he was standing pissing off the side of the platform, I crept along and gave him a gigantic shove and he really was out of his tree. Crash.

13TH NOVEMBER 2040

I've wrapped your remains in my good blue shirt; sorry I couldn't let you stay on board, but there's no future now for any baby above ground. I'm the end of the line!

This is the last page of my thirtieth-birthday present. When I've finished it I'll wrap the notebook up in six plastic bags, sealing each one with duct tape against the rain, then I'll bury it in a hole on top of the blue shirt. I don't know why as I'm not mad enough to think anybody will ever read it. After that I'm going to buckle on this rucksack of provisions and head north with my gun. Wish me luck. Last line: good luck, good luck, good luck, good luck, good luck.

Charm for a Friend with a Lump

First let me take a piece of chalk and draw a circle round you, so you're safe. There. Now I'll stand guard, keeping a weather eye open for anything threatening, and we can catch up with each other while we wait.

Have a glance through this garden catalog if you would. I need your help in choosing what to plant this spring. I thought the little yellow Peacevine tomatoes, so sweet and sharp, along with Gardener's Delight and Tiger Toms; but there's a lot to be said for Marmande too.

I'll have a word with the powers-that-be. The Health Czar. Ban parabens. I'll keep away the spotted snakes with double tongues, I'll be like Cobweb and Mustardseed in the play; I'll make sure the beetles black approach not near. By naming the bad things I'll haul them up into the light and shrivel their power over you. Hence, malignant tumor, hence; carcinoma, come not here.

Then I thought I'd try those stripy round zucchinis this year, Ronds de Nice. You have to pick them as soon as they reach the size of tennis balls, you mustn't let them get any bigger than that or they won't be worth eating. They'll swell and grow as big as footballs if you let them. As for fruit, what do you think of Conference pears? Or the catalog recommends the Invincible, a very hardy variety that crops heavily and blooms twice a year.

Let's not even start on those predictable but useless paths which lead to nowhere. If only I hadn't smoked at fifteen, if only there hadn't been that betrayal, if only I hadn't spent so much time putting up with the insupportable—why ever did I think endurance was a virtue? Didn't I *want* to stay alive? If only I hadn't sipped wine, or drunk water from plastic bottles. If only I hadn't gone jogging the day Chernobyl exploded. Oh, give it a rest! We live in the world as it is, we all have to breathe its contagious fogs. It's wrong of them to claim it must somehow be our own fault when our health is under attack.

Let's get back to the catalog. Help me choose some soft fruit. If I had more space I might try gooseberries again now there's this new cultivar that cheats American blight. But it's probably wiser to add to the existing black currant patch; here's a new one, Titania, "large fruit and good flavor. Crops very heavily over a long period. Good resistance to mildew and rust."

We're advised to build up an arsenal of elixirs if we want to strengthen our own resistance. We're told we ought to call in light boxes, amulets, echinacea drops and oily fish, we should fix on organic free-range grass-fed meat, Japanese green tea and a daily dose of turmeric. And if we're really serious about protecting ourselves we must avoid dry cleaners, getting fat, aluminium, insecticides; shun trans fats as the devil's food; forswear polystyrene cups. We've got to fight shy of white bread, a sedentary lifestyle, perfume and anger, if we truly want to save ourselves. And even if we check off every item on the list, there's absolutely no guarantee that it'll lengthen our span by a single day.

On your last birthday, with your natural dislike of being reminded of the passing years, we skirted round the subject for a while. I asked what you'd be doing to celebrate. You scoffed. You said you'd rather forget about it. Do you remember? Then I reached down into myself and managed to say, "You *should* celebrate, your birthday *should* be celebrated, because the world's a better place with you in it." May you continue to pile on the years, but with more pleasure from now on.

In time may you embrace fallen arches and age spots; decades from now may your joints creak and your ears hiss, may your crow's-feet laugh back into the mirror at your quivering dewlaps.

Nobody in their right mind looks at an old oak tree growing in strength and richness and thinks, You'll be dead soon. They just admire and draw strength from its example. May you keep your hair on and your eyebrows in place. May you never have to wear a hat indoors. May you and your other half tuck two centuries under your belts between you and then, like the old couple in the tale, when some kind god in disguise grants you a wish, may you go together, hand in hand, in an instant.

I'm willing you to be well. Do you hear me? If there does happen to be some disorder in your blood, I'm like Canute—I'll stay here by you and turn the tide. You're my persona grata.

And if they find that some weed or canker has gained hold after all—Japanese knotweed, it might be, that ruthless invader and ignorer of boundaries—well, then, we'll deal with it. There are powerful new weed killers these days, and they work. Doctors are like gardeners in the way they know how to distinguish between healthy growth and uncontrollable proliferation. There's a fine line, and what I am casting a spell for is that nothing inside you has stepped over it.

In my spell we are dreaming our way forward

through the year into the green and white of May, and on into the deep green lily ponds of June. The lushness of June, its new heat and subdued glitter of excitement at dusk, its scent and roses, that's what we'll aim for. I do love roses, their scent and beauty, particularly my Souvenir du Dr. Jamain and the thorny pink eglantine beside the vegetable patch.

We'll have a party there this Midsummer's Eve, up by the tomato plants and ranks of romaine lettuce, just the two of us. Let's write it on our calendars now. I can't spare you. You're indispensable! We'll have a party and pledge your health by moonlight on the one night of the year when plants consumed or planted have magical powers.

There is a great deal of talk about the benefits of mistletoe extract and so on, but I'm not convinced. You can spend a lot of time and energy chasing magic potions, when you might be better occupied weaving your own spells over the future. En route, sleep will help. Everyone has their own private walled garden at night where they can prune their troubles and dream change into some sort of shape. That's what I'm trying to say: a dream can be a transformer, as well as providing a margin or grassy bank where you can rest while the outside world goes on. Active dreaming, which is what I would prescribe, can be a powerful form of enchantment.

You're not out of the woods yet, that's clear; but a

little while from now I want you to walk out of the woods and into the June garden. Leave the black bats hanging upside down; they'll stay asleep. While we wait for summer, let's choose to be patient and hopeful. And soon, not really long from now at all, I aim to smile at you and say, Come into the garden, friend of my heart.

A NOTE ON THE TYPE

*The text of this book was set in Garamond No. 3. It is
not a true copy of any of the designs of Claude Garamond
(ca. 1480–1561) but an adaptation of his types, which
set the European standard for two centuries. This particular
version is based on an adaptation by Morris Fuller Benton.*

TYPESET BY *North Market Street Graphics, Lancaster, Pennsylvania*

PRINTED AND BOUND BY *Thomson-Shore, Dexter, Michigan*

DESIGNED BY *Iris Weinstein*